REPOSSESSED

Also by A. M. Jenkins

Breaking Boxes

Damage

Out of Order

Beating Heart: A Ghost Story

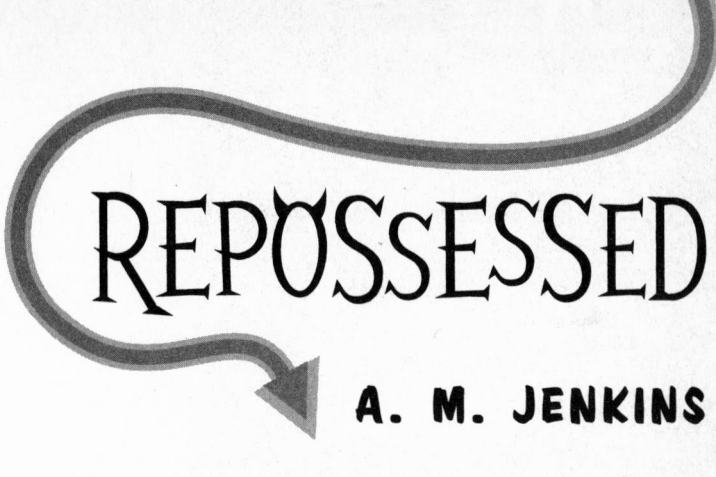

REPOSSESSED

A. M. JENKINS

HARPERTEEN

An Imprint of HarperCollins*Publishers*

*To my editor, Anne Hoppe, for her
diligence, insight, and trust, and for not letting
me get away with less than my best*

HarperTeen is an imprint of HarperCollins Publishers.

Repossessed
Text copyright © 2007 by A. M. Jenkins
All rights reserved. Printed in the United States of
America. No part of this book may be used or reproduced
in any manner whatsoever without written permission
except in the case of brief quotations embodied in critical
articles and reviews. For information address HarperCollins
Children's Books, a division of HarperCollins Publishers,
1350 Avenue of the Americas, New York, NY 10019.
www.harperteen.com

Library of Congress Cataloging-in-Publication Data is available.
ISBN-10: 0-06-083568-0 (trade bdg.)
ISBN-13: 978-0-06-083568-2 (trade bdg.)
ISBN-10: 0-06-083569-9 (lib. bdg.)
ISBN-13: 978-0-06-083569-9 (lib. bdg.)

Typography by Jennifer Heuer
1 2 3 4 5 6 7 8 9 10
❖
First Edition

Acknowledgments

Thanks to my friends Cathy Atkins, Kris Cliff-Evans, Lisa Firke, Shirley Harazin, Cindy Lord, Nancy Werlin, Laura Wiess, and Melissa Wyatt for their critiques and support. Also to the Four Star group for all their help over the summer: David Davis, Chris Ford, Trish Holland, Kathy Lay, Tom McDermott, Jan Peck, Diane Roberts, Sue Ward, and Cerelle Woods. A very special thank-you to my writing buddy Martha Moore, who's always there for me, and to Steve Malk, whose hard work and dedication enable me to continue writing.

First thing I did was, I stole a body. I could have made my own, but I wasn't in an artistic frame of mind.

I was just fed up, you know; fed up with being a cog in a vast machine, with doing my pointless, demeaning job. It's not like I was the only one who could do it—*anybody* could do it. Tormenting the damned—it practically does itself, no lie. And it's depressing; I can't tell you how depressing it is.

I didn't tell the Boss, didn't tell anyone I was going. No, Hell could get along just fine without me.

As for the Creator, the One—if you ask me, He hasn't ever paid the place much notice. He wound the watch up, set the hands, and let it start ticking.

Really, the Creator is the one I have the grievance

with. Not the Boss. The Boss is just doing his job like the rest of us, just fulfilling his function. The Creator is the one who set up all the rules. And now He never checks in, doesn't seem to know or care whether the peons of Hell are getting overworked and fed up. I've never been fool enough to expect redemption, but even a tiny spark of recognition of my drudging toil—or even my mere *existence*—would have been nice. For thousands upon thousands of years I've labored under a slowly fading hope.

After a while, it was just too much. Even a being like me—no, *especially* a being like me—has its breaking point.

So. The hard part was picking a body. I wanted to keep it simple, start small. Slip into a life that was already taking place. Something with all the synapses in working condition. A body that was carefree, insulated from earthly considerations like hunger; a protected place to try out physical existence. A body without responsibilities—no job or family to care for; someone who had time to experience the things I wanted to experience. But not *too* protected. Someone who wasn't watched every second. Someone who had a little time on his hands, but also a safe place to go to every night.

I knew I wanted all this, so I decided to take a middle-class suburban American teenager. I looked around for a bit and found a few that I observed closely, waiting until one turned up good to go.

The actual hijacking of the body took place about one second before the guy was about to step out from behind a parked SUV into the street and get iced, as they say, by a speeding cement mixer. My candidates were all slackers, you see, not too quick on the uptake, and this one was talking to his friend and stepped off the curb without looking—or started to. The fact that he missed the last two seconds of his life didn't really matter; I could see exactly what was going to happen. And although technically there's free will and anything could have interfered with his death, like a timely muscle cramp to make him pause on the curb—or heck, a bird could have been flying over-head and suddenly taken ill in midair and fallen on his head and knocked him out the second before he stepped into the street—there are laws of physics, and trust me, after millions of millennia, I can spot an inevitability.

Body-snatching is pretty rare amongst my kind. Tech-nically speaking, I broke a few rules, but what are they going to do? Send me to Hell, ha ha?

Anyway, he stepped out into space and I jerked his foot back, and there I was on the curb while he was mak-ing his whooshy tunnel-of-light way to the hereafter.

All at once I was in this brand-new, slightly used body. It was a fast-motion fill-up, like pouring myself all at once into a too-tight vessel. I'm not used to boundaries, and to be suddenly constricted—to need to breathe, to have a beginning and an end—gave me a feeling of . . . well, almost panic.

But then everything else flooded in and I was swimming in a vast sea of sensory information. I wasn't expecting it, and it threw me into confusion. I'd been expecting to just take over, smooth and unnoticed—it looks so easy to be human, considering that they're all a little dim—but suddenly I could see, hear, feel. It was beautiful.

Everything was beautiful.

"Shaun, you okay?" said Shaun's best friend, Bailey. I looked at him through Shaun's eyes, and it was the weirdest thing.

I have never been anything but spirit—anywhere and everywhere I wanted to be, just never in a physical sense. This was the first time I was ever in exactly *one* place. Before, I could have known what anybody on earth was doing, if I'd felt like it. I wouldn't have been able to see or hear what they were doing, but I would have been *aware* of it. Sort of an amorphous cloud with the ability to inhabit many discrete sites at once.

But now, in a human body, I was immersed in an ocean of details. Every single one of them was crisp, clear, and distinct. I was overwhelmed, so even though I had exactly *one* person—Bailey—in my field of vision, I only had a dim, muffled idea of what his facial expression and body language might mean, and I had to think really hard to try and remember a human American word for what I thought Bailey might be feeling right now.

Taking on a body, it seemed, was constricting in more ways than one.

"I'm okay," I answered, feeling the sound rolling out of my throat like a wave. It was so thrilling, I did it again. "I'm okay," I told Bailey, and I looked at the way his irises had bright color, a bluish gray. Color—what a concept! What a wonderful thing to see, what a great creation! I had to give the Creator a tip of the hat on that one.

Maybe that's why He never checks on Hell. I didn't realize how intricate, how *rich*, earthly perception was. Could be He was busy with the day-to-day here; either that or He was still resting up from setting all this into motion.

Now I was starting to grasp even more of the details. As I looked around at all the movement, heard noises big and small, felt the warmth of the sun—what a coup, the sun! what a terrifyingly beautiful thing to come up with! again, tip of the hat!—and the faint coolness of a breeze that I couldn't see, I knew I couldn't just pick up in the middle of Shaun's day and carry on as Shaun had planned. I had to go back to his house; be alone for some quiet time; get used to this body, this space, this existence.

I wanted to go someplace where nobody could see,

and do stuff like make different noises with my throat and tongue, and pick up things with my fingers, and look at the bottoms of my feet and at my genitalia.

"You sure you're okay?" Bailey asked with a sort of squint to his eyes and a slightly wrinkled forehead, and I remembered that he and Shaun had been heading to Bailey's house, as was their habit, and that since I was taking Shaun's place, I'd better give a reason for changing plans all of a sudden.

"I'm not feeling too good," I told Bailey. "My stomach hurts." I thought that was quite a realistic touch. Humans do have stomachaches; they have them all the time. "I'm going to go home and lie down for a minute."

"Want me to go with you?"

"No, no," I said, and in a flash of brilliance I added, "Must have been the burrito." Because that's what Shaun had for lunch, a burrito from the school cafeteria.

"Dude, I told you not to eat that thing."

"Shut up," I said happily. That's what Shaun and Bailey say to each other all the time: *shut up*. Oh, I was really sliding into the groove!

"Well," Bailey said, turning away, "if you get to feeling better, come on over."

"Okay," I said, still happy, and I started walking off in the opposite direction.

Or tried to. Shaun's legs went to rubber, a confusion

of too many joints, too many muscles and tendons that had to be placed at exact angles. All the while keeping his body upright, his head at the very top of this moving column.

I found myself dipping and weaving and, for a moment, stumbling forward in an effort to remain on Shaun's feet and earn the name *Homo erectus* at the very least.

It took a good half a block for me to get a rhythm going, but it was pure fun trying. Having sight didn't help at first, because everything around me rushed toward and past Shaun's eyes at varying rates, depending on its distance from his body. Finally I fixed his gaze on the asphalt a few feet ahead of him, and concentrated on how it *felt* to move his legs. Once I got them going, I marveled at the way they were able to coordinate in perfect rhythm—one miscue and he'd go down in a heap, but no, it was as smooth as if he'd been born walking, so smooth it was downright miraculous.

Then I noticed that with proper leg motions, his arms naturally began to swing slightly, alternating. Somehow this made balancing easier.

I was walking!

Creator, I thought, *I'm sorry I didn't understand what a bang-up job You did on this place.*

He didn't answer, of course.

I turned Shaun's head from side to side, taking in all my surroundings, and soon I found that fast movement of this kind made Shaun's eyes perceive things as a blur. So I stopped on the sidewalk and turned around a few times to watch the world lose its form as it passed by. When I stopped, I had a wild sensation that I was still spinning, so much so that I lost my balance again and staggered. When I finally was able to stand up straight and focus, I found that I was facing back the way I'd come from, facing Bailey.

He wasn't looking at me; he was heading up the hill to his house.

I watched his back for a moment, the way *he* walked. I'd never understood before that humans walked in different ways, even though their speed and length of stride might be essentially the same. Bailey had a lanky, loose-kneed kind of step. It was clear to see, now.

As I stood there, watching with great interest, I realized I could identify what Bailey had been feeling when I took over Shaun's body.

Concern, that's what it was.

I don't like the term "demon." It carries quite a bit of negativity with it. It implies a pointy tail and cloven hooves. I prefer the term "fallen angel." That is, indeed, what we are. The difference between us and the angels who didn't fall from grace is that the Unfallen were, are, and always will be faithful, stalwart, and obedient. That is their nature, just as it is their nature to rejoice in worship and contemplation of the vastness of the Creator's perfection. We, the Fallen, wondered, questioned, confronted, eventually demanded, and in general pushed the edges of the envelope till the envelope burst.

Since the Creator knows all in the vastness of time, you may ask yourself whether we the Fallen are merely carrying out our part in His plan. That *is* a question.

Good luck getting an answer. His thoughts, His ultimate designs are mysteries. Except to—maybe—the Unfallen. I've never been sure about that, because the Unfallen don't hang out with us peons much anymore.

I've never really liked those guys.

I went to Shaun's house, eager to check out this body that was now mine. On the way, I kept looking up at the vastness of sky. Oh, what a blue! And the clouds moved, not just in one direction, but rushing, tumbling, rolling, redefining themselves every second.

I felt Shaun's mouth stretching, and lifted his hands to touch his face. His fingers encountered small, squarish hard things.

Teeth. I was grinning! That was wonderful, too—facial muscles reflecting emotions, which are some of the most intangible things in existence. What an exquisite world this was! I should have come here sooner.

On Shaun's porch, I took the key from his pocket and unlocked his front door.

Shaun's parents were divorced. That was one reason I'd picked this body—less supervision. His father was out of town at the moment. His mother, with whom he lived, was at work right now, but his little brother would be here, home from school. I knew the brother, of course, as I knew everyone Shaun came into contact with, but I couldn't wait to see him through physical eyes.

Not that Shaun would have thought twice about Jason. I'd been watching Shaun quite closely for a while, and it was obvious that when Shaun felt anything about his brother at all, it was annoyance at a "pain in the butt" and a "pest." And Shaun's brother often expressed anger at Shaun for being "bossy" and "mean."

I already knew more than I wanted to know about human annoyance and anger. I'd spent most of my existence buried under the endless drone of negativity that envelops every one of the billions of my, shall we say, *clients*. Most of them are in my charge not because of what they did, but because of what they didn't do. There's some kind of interaction with the Creator—which of course I'm not privy to—and the souls come, slathered in guilt and regrets. There they remain, to agonize and anguish.

The only uplifting times are when, usually after millennia of suffering, a single soul suddenly, for no reason that's apparent to me, decides that it's had enough, that it's paid the price for its wrongs, and it sort of twists itself inside out, shedding its misery to go free. It's a beautiful, memorable, and very rare event. It's a cool rush, a sweet atom of a moment in an eternity of heavy dark. But even that fine moment has its bitterness. In Hell, nothing is pure joy. There's sorrow in the moment of release, when the soul realizes that a true sin, once committed, can never be undone, and thus in one respect can never be paid for.

How the length of the soul's stay is decided, I have no idea. I've wondered often enough. I know the kind of reckoning *I* had, after the Rebellion. It wasn't a trial with judgment pronounced from on high. More like the peeling back of the outer layers of one's being, all protection ripped off, leaving one with an excruciating, painfully naked self-appraisal. When that was over, I knew what my punishment was. I knew it would have no end. No one told me. I just *knew*.

Is it the same way with souls? Do they have to serve a prearranged sentence imposed upon them by the Creator? Or do they know on their own when they've atoned for whatever they did or neglected to do?

Whatever the reason, they punish themselves. I merely oversee; I don't actively *do* anything *about* anything.

Mine is a useless occupation.

As I let myself into Shaun's house, I wondered how long it'd take the powers that be to care that I was no longer doing my job. In any case, I was going to enjoy every second of this holiday while I could.

I pulled the door shut behind me. Shaun's cat was in the entry, next to the front door, sunning itself on the windowsill. I was instantly curious; many people love their pets more than they love other humans, and

I've always wondered why.

As far as I have been able to see, animals don't give much to their owners; they let themselves be fed and petted, which has always seemed to me to be entirely a matter of self-interest. Now I observed that this cat did look very soft. It might feel pleasing under the fingertips. Perhaps stroking it might be the key to the pet-owner relationship.

But as I approached, Shaun's cat—its name was Peanut—leaped up, hissing, ears flat, and backed away. I stopped. "Kittykittykitty," I called, as humans do, while bending slightly to hold one hand out for the cat to sniff.

The cat turned and ran. It disappeared down the hall.

Did it know I wasn't Shaun?

I stood up. I didn't see how the cat *could* know. It wasn't as if I smelled different.

I'd just have to try again later.

I stepped out of the entryway, into the living room. Shaun's little brother, Jason, sat on the floor in front of the TV, playing a video game. He was a compact and complex bundle, in person. The hairs on his head were smooth and appeared to be one shining entity, when I knew there had to be hundreds of thousands of them. His body was relaxed except for his hands, which gripped a controller, and his fingers, which seemed to spasm in tiny movements: tapping, pushing, pulling, circling.

Shaun does not normally greet his brother; in fact, he ignores his existence most of the time. But I wanted to interact, and I liked the feel of Shaun's voice rumbling out of his chest, and I enjoyed making the changes in tongue, throat, and lips that enabled speech.

"Hey, jerkwad," I said pleasantly, because this was how Shaun always addressed his brother.

"Shut up," said Jason without looking around. He did not say it with the same lazy, innocuous meaning that Shaun and Bailey used. He loaded the two syllables with loathing and resentment.

I was glad to have been able to exchange speech with another human, and went humming into Shaun's room.

There I stopped in the doorway to take it all in. Or tried to.

Shaun's mother says his room is one big pit without any organization whatsoever, but the truth is that Shaun has a system. He drops the dirty clothes on the floor when he takes them off, and tosses the clean ones on the bed and chair and doorknob. He does not make his bed because, he says, he will only mess it up again that night. His CDs are not in order, and they are on the floor rather than in the rack his father bought him, but they *are* in stacks. Mostly. He knows where they are in general, if not specifically. Dirty dishes lie on the bedside table because Shaun only makes a dish run whenever his trash can is full. Then he takes all his plates and glasses to the kitchen as he carries the trash out.

However, there is no question that Shaun's room is a mess. In fact, I only fully comprehended what a "mess" was when I saw Shaun's room. Everything blurred and seemed to run together—the colors, the textures, the shapes. It was . . . unpleasant. Not in and of itself, but because I couldn't separate out something to experience.

Finally I bent and picked up a T-shirt. The words on the front were faded, and scaling from having been washed. I drew the shirt through his fingers, feeling the slight stretch of the material. Wonderful. Soft. I crumpled the shirt in Shaun's hand and watched it take on shadows in the folds. Then I lifted it and gently brushed the material against Shaun's cheek. It felt even softer—interesting, how the more sensitive fingers have slightly different perceptions from the face, which has fewer nerve endings.

The lips have almost as many nerve endings as the fingers. I shut Shaun's eyes and rubbed the shirt against his lips. Now it didn't really feel soft at all, but rough, and as I held it there, a sour stench rose into my borrowed nostrils and I realized that this shirt smelled like three-day-old sweat from Shaun's armpits.

"What are you *doing*?"

I jumped. It's the startle reflex; even infants have it. I didn't know how disagreeable it was.

I looked up to see Shaun's brother in the open doorway. Jason's eyes were a lovely color, sort of a pale green. I doubted that many people had observed this; Jason was renowned for his lack of eye contact.

Then I realized that what Jason saw now was Shaun standing in the middle of the room, eyes shut, while he slowly rubbed a stinky T-shirt over his mouth.

I would have known, even if I hadn't seen the expression on Jason's face, that he thought this behavior odd.

"Nothing," I told him. That's what Shaun would have said, even if Shaun would never have been feeling his own clothes with his lips.

"Jerkwad," I added, as an afterthought. Somehow, though, I had missed the rhythm of conversation. Jason did not say "Shut up." He did not move.

"Are you making out with your *shirt*?"

I wasn't interested in what Jason thought of me. What I was interested in was Shaun's tongue.

The tongue has even more nerve endings than the fingers or lips. I wondered what the material would feel like against my tongue, how it would differ from what I'd already experienced.

Still, I thought carefully, to reason out what Shaun would have done about Jason. I hoped to lie low during my sojourn, whether it ended up being minutes or hours.

"Get out of my room," I told him, as Shaun would

have, and stepped toward the door.

"I'm not in your room."

"Get out of my doorway," I told him, and shut the door in his face.

3

Most of the "sins" that keep people in Hell are—in my opinion—entirely natural and entirely petty. For example, Envy. It's a rare person indeed who doesn't feel a twinge of jealousy when a friend achieves something the person hasn't.

Or Sloth. Only a few times in my career have I seen a soul who hasn't taken a moment to lie around while someone else does a bit more of the work.

But from the way souls whine and moan around the afterlife, you'd think that Sloth and Envy were biggies, equal to murder. Why do they call them the Seven Deadly Sins? I couldn't tell you. And I have no influence on any of the souls I supervise, so I never have any choice but to watch these idiots torturing themselves for lifetimes over what seem to be the most inconsequential things.

But now I had a body. Now I got to experience some sin in the physical sense, see what it was all about. Envy, Sloth, Pride, Greed, Gluttony, Wrath, and Lust. As well as anything else I could think of. Starting small, of course—the whole point of the Shaun episode was to start small, with manageable moments, in order to ease into the experience, and also in the hope that I wouldn't draw immediate attention from the higher-ups.

I already knew that I wanted to try one of the little "sins" that comes up the most often. It haunts so many, many souls in some form or fashion that I have always wanted to see why it is so shrouded in excitement and guilt.

It is clear to me that masturbation is natural. Even apes do it. Why is it a big deal to so many people?

And if it's so awful, why do they *keep doing it*?

I knew what it was, of course, how it worked—I knew so many odd permutations of the act that it would have made Shaun's brain reel if he had still been in charge of said brain—but I just wanted to try the basic, most common method.

One of Shaun's habits was to do it in the shower, so I decided to stick with that. At first, anyway.

I went into the bathroom, turned on the water,

stripped down, and climbed in.

Then I leaped back out. I'd forgotten the part where Shaun adjusts the temperature.

While I waited for the water to heat up, I examined Shaun's face in the mirror. His hair hung over his forehead and in his eyes; I lifted it with one hand to get a better look. His eyes were a nondescript color that might have been hazel or gray. There was a white scar on his forehead that he'd received from falling off a swing when he was a child. I'd never heard him say why he chose to wear his hair in his face, but now I wondered if he was trying to hide the scar.

I rather *liked* it. How wonderful, to bear evidence of an event that must have been packed with emotion! How satisfying, to always have a physical token of something you'd experienced.

I checked out his body as well. He was too thin, in my opinion. No, not too thin, exactly—he'd just look more appealing to me and probably everyone else if he did something besides sitting around playing video games. I knew he would have felt better, too. It's been clear to me that Shaun has always felt inadequate about his build. Especially his chest and arms.

I turned this way and that. He had no muscular definition, that was for sure. There was a weight bench in his room—under several pairs of jeans, a torn backpack, and an old blanket—but he'd only used it a few times and then quit.

I thought I'd try the weight bench out, perhaps after I masturbated, or after dinner. I was curious as to why so many people commit themselves to an exercise program and then quit. And why they then act as if they feel *guilty* about quitting. And the whole time, they behave as though they're ashamed of their bodies. That whole process has never made sense to me.

I stuck Shaun's hand under the showerhead to check the temperature. The water felt good now. I never knew how soothing, how voluptuous, running water could be.

As I stepped into the shower and pulled the curtain behind me, I began to feel a delicious excitement. Shaun's body parts felt it, too; they began to fill with anticipation.

They knew what I was about to do to them.

And I did it. Oh boy, did I do it.

When the shower was over, I was gasping and Shaun's heart was racing. I couldn't see why humans didn't do it even *more* often than they did. Heck, I would have wondered why they didn't do it all day *long* if I didn't know that there are other parts of the psyche that need fulfillment besides the sexual drive.

However, I could now understand why this feeling has given rise (pardon the pun) to more obsessions than any other aspect of human existence.

I had also decided that I probably should have started with a different body. Now I wanted to try sex with another person. I already *knew* what sex was, in great and florid detail, but now I was determined to *feel* it.

First lesson learned: *Knowing* doesn't hold a candle to *doing*.

One problem with Shaun was that he had no regular sexual partner. In fact, he had no sexual partner whatsoever. Worst of all, he had no prospect of one. He was heterosexual but had no girlfriend and no friends who were girls. I wished now I'd picked someone who was already having regular sexual activity.

But after only a short time, I already felt an attachment to this particular body, to this particular life. Good old Shaun; I'd never seen any clue that he appreciated the wonder shining in every one of his moments. I thought I'd known everything about him, but living life through his body made what I knew seem dull and one-dimensional. I liked seeing the eyes of his friend and his brother, and I wanted to see more. Humans were much more intriguing from this point of view. They were like puzzles waiting to be put together, mysteries to be solved.

No, being Shaun was fun enough. For now, I'd just try to have sex in his body. It shouldn't be difficult. I'd try a girl first—the most common human sexual experience, to start with: vaginal intercourse between male and female.

It was only too bad that Shaun wasn't here to experience all the things I was going to do with this body. He would have loved it.

After I finished the shower, I filled up the tub and took a bath. I filled it as high as it would go. I liked this water; I liked the feeling of it. It was warm and floaty. I slapped the surface to make little waves that disappeared quickly, and then I slid Shaun's whole body back and forth to make big waves that slopped over the side of the tub. When the water got cold, I filled the tub again, with even hotter water that turned Shawn's skin red. I watched his fingers and toes prune up.

I lay back so that his ears were under the surface, and I listened to his skin squeak as I rubbed his legs and bottom along the porcelain. Then I knocked on the side of the tub and listened to the echoing clank.

Cool.

When I sat up, water draining out of Shaun's ears, I heard a woman's voice. "He's been in there *how* long?"

Shaun's mom.

I listened, rivulets running down Shaun's back and chest.

"Two and a half hours." That was Jason. "Every time I knock, he just says he's taking a bath."

Well, I *was* taking a bath.

Footsteps.

Knock knock knock.

"Shaun, baby?" His mom sounded worried. "You all right?"

"Just fine," I called out. But now I was thinking that maybe I *had* been in a bit long, for a human. For Shaun. The water was cold again, anyway; his arms were goose-pimply. "I'm getting out now," I called to Shaun's mother.

I let the water out of the tub while I dried off; then I wrapped a towel around Shaun's waist. The air was a lot colder than the water had been; it was uncomfortable. Still, being curious, I opened the medicine cabinet and poked around in it a bit, reading all the labels on the bottles and boxes. AQuify. Target brand ibuprofen. Benadryl.

Hmm. Maybe Shaun would get sick so I could experience a runny nose, sneezing, and itchy, watery eyes, and then feel them being relieved by the medication. I especially wanted to try a sneeze. I'd never quite understood what one was. It seemed like it would be painful—the forceful and sudden expulsion of air through one's nose—but generally, no one seemed to be hurt by it.

I shut the cabinet door, then slid open a drawer and looked inside.

"Shaun?" His mom's voice again. This time it sounded as if she was right up against the door. "I'm beginning to get a little worried. Do I need to come in there?"

"No, I'll be out in a sec," I told her calmly, popping the lid off Shaun's stick deodorant. I rolled the little wheel to make more deodorant come out. Then I rolled it back. Rolled it out again. Interesting.

I remembered the stench of Shaun's T-shirt, and rubbed some under his arms. It didn't feel like much of anything. I sniffed the stick. Right Guard Xtreme Power Stripe; it smelled good.

When I finally opened the bathroom door, Shaun's mom was discreetly sitting in the living room, in the only chair that allowed a clear sight line to the bathroom door. She doesn't normally sit there. She doesn't normally sit at all when she comes home from work; usually she changes clothes and starts a load of laundry.

I felt a short surge of affection for her. She was trying hard not to be a pushy parent.

She looked up when I came out, and her eyes widened. Then she turned away quickly.

Shaun never steps out of the bathroom unless he's fully dressed. But I'd forgotten to take clean clothes in with me, and so I was wearing only a small, damp towel.

This time when I went into Shaun's room, I remembered to shut the door behind me. I dropped the towel on the floor and looked toward some of Shaun's clean clothes that he'd left draped over the electric guitar he never plays. But now that I had gotten somewhat used to the feel of cloth against Shaun's skin, I was dissatisfied with the way his clothes looked. Raggedy. Limp. Faded. Full of holes. I knew Shaun fought every time his mom tried to take him shopping, but I'd never thought about what that meant.

His mom did take him shopping, every year before school started. Against his will, she always bought him clothes that he never wore. This year's were still hanging in the closet, with the price tags on.

Those were what I wanted to wear. If they still fit. Shaun being a growing boy and all.

I found a shirt in the closet and pulled it on. Then pants. Shaun's ratty old clothes had felt better against my skin, soft and worn. But these unworn clothes had a bright crispness about them that pleased me a great deal.

I looked at myself in Shaun's mirror. His hair needed

a trim, I thought, to reveal more of his face, but otherwise I had him looking pretty snappy.

I turned and looked at myself from various angles, and felt even more pleased. Was this Pride? Or Vanity?

Whatever it was, it felt *good*.

I watched myself in Shaun's mirror as I tucked his shirt in, then inserted a belt through the loops at his waist and buckled it.

That didn't look right to me. The shirt was a lovely blue, conversely brighter *and* darker than the sky. But almost half of it was now hidden under the pants. And the belt seemed like a torture device intended to bind the shirt tightly in its pants prison, offering no chance of escape.

I took off the belt and untucked. *Go free, little shirt!*

Shaun's shoes were smelly and mildewed, and I didn't want them on his nicely cleaned feet, so I dug around in the closet and found some shoes that he wore to a wedding a few months ago.

"Shaun, old boy," I whispered to the mirror as I combed his hair, "I wish you could see yourself."

When I came out of the room, Shaun's mother's mouth dropped open.

"Are you going somewhere?" was all she asked.

"I don't think so," I told her. "I wasn't planning to."

"Oh," she said in a small voice. "You look nice," she

added tentatively, after a moment.

"Thank you," I said.

I sat on the couch and watched Jason play a video game. I was not interested in playing any myself, but now, looking through Shaun's eyes, I could see that Jason was actually very good. He shot his way through many aliens, then collected a health pickup that erased what minimal damage he'd sustained.

At first he kept looking at me over his shoulder, as if I were about to attack him from behind. But then he forgot about me and just played.

Dinner was fairly silent. Both Jason and Shaun's mom kept darting looks at me. Shaun's mom had made hot dogs, and they were delicious. I had one with mustard, one with cheese and ketchup, one with relish and mustard and ketchup and cheese. I decided I liked the ketchup best, and ate a bun with just that on it. Was this Gluttony? I hoped so. I certainly was enjoying it.

I saw Shaun's mom open her mouth a few times to say something, but each time nothing came out and she closed her mouth again.

Finally she managed to speak. "Shaun," she said, "are you sure you're feeling all right?"

"Yes," I told her, "I'm fine." At the same moment, I realized that I had forgotten to put on any underwear. No matter. I took another bun, opened it, and put ketchup on it.

"He's psycho," Jason told her. "He was French-kissing his shirt earlier."

I started to object that I had not "French-kissed" anything. But then I remembered how I'd felt the T-shirt with various parts of my tongue after I shut the door in Jason's face, and so I remained silent while I ate my bun.

"Jason, you are not being helpful," his mom said. "Shaun . . . did something happen today? Anything out of the ordinary?"

Well, Shaun died, but other than that . . .

"Nope," I told Shaun's mom. "It's just been a normal, regular day."

"Okay." She looked puzzled, watching me stuff the last of the ketchupy bun into my mouth. "Anyway, I'm glad you're finally wearing the clothes I bought you." Something flickered across her face, and suddenly she seemed to relax. She didn't say anything. But I saw her smile secretly to herself.

"Have you boys done your homework yet?" she asked, getting up to clear the table.

"No," said Jason.

"No," I said.

"Will you please get it done before you go to bed?"

Jason sighed. I thought about it for a moment. Shaun did bring his backpack home, and in it was a biology worksheet that was due tomorrow. Of course, he'd left all his books at the bottom of his locker.

It didn't matter. I knew all the answers. And I thought it would be fun to read questions and let the answers form themselves into actual words inside Shaun's head. And to write, on a piece of paper, with a pencil—to experience for myself the delicacy of finger movements required to make marks that communicated one's thoughts to anyone who saw them. Sounded like fun to me!

"I'll do it right now," I told Shaun's mom.

It *was* fun. I sharpened the pencil in Shaun's electric sharpener—buzz, buzz, and it's done!—and laid my cheek on the paper to watch the thready trail of graphite left behind as I formed the letters. Then I erased some to watch the graphite roll away in little pink particles. Then I switched to ballpoint pen. That wasn't as much fun, so I went to get a gel pen and swooped along the lines in cursive rather than in printing. Finally I put Shaun's name at the top in block letters and drew shadows hanging from them so they looked 3-D. Cool.

I put the finished homework in Shaun's backpack. Then I cleared the clothes off Shaun's weight bench to try lifting weights. I folded the clothes and put them in a drawer, because I didn't like having to kick everything aside just to walk.

After a few go-rounds with the weight bench, I still couldn't see why Shaun had quit. I liked the way it made his arms feel stretchy. He'd started with heavier weights than I did; maybe that was it. I remembered that he had seemed bored, and couldn't make himself stick with it. But it was only a few minutes a day. I didn't get it. I've always *known* why humans do certain things, but I've never really *understood* a lot of it.

I put the weights down and started picking up Shaun's dirty clothes. I wanted them out of the room. I didn't care for the way they smelled. I liked the clothes that smelled faintly of laundry detergent.

I headed to the laundry room, carrying the pile of clothes. When I passed through the living room, Jason was sitting on the floor in front of the coffee table, books and papers scattered all over it. He was hunched over his work, and something about him looked different. I paused to observe him for a moment to figure it out.

He sighed loudly, flipped through a few pages, wrote a few words. Then he sighed again and ran his fingers through his hair.

That was it. He had been absentmindedly using his fingers as a rake, so that now his hair stuck straight up in odd tufts and spikes on his head. Before, it had been lying down, following the shape of his skull.

As I watched, his pencil stopped moving and he turned his head to look at me. I noticed that in this light, at this distance, I could not see the lovely color of his irises.

I turned away with Shaun's dirty clothes, and continued to the laundry room.

As I dumped Shaun's clothes into the basket, I heard Jason's voice coming faintly from down the hall. "Mom," he said, "is something wrong with Shaun?"

"Shh. He'll hear you." Her voice was low. "He's just growing up."

"But did you see what he was *wearing*?"

"It's normal for a teenage boy to take a sudden interest in his appearance. And did you hear him lifting weights?"

"So?"

I heard her sigh. "It's a *girl*, Jason. Shaun is interested in a girl."

"Who?"

"I don't know," Shaun's mom said quietly, "but I have a good guess."

I walked back through the room and they both got quiet suddenly. Jason bent over his homework again. Shaun's mom, however looked up and gave me a pleasant smile.

I stopped and smiled back at her. Then I went on to Shaun's room.

Lady, I thought as I shut the door behind me, *it's a mercy that you don't have a clue.*

5

Kyrie eleison. It's Greek, meaning "Lord have mercy." I've always liked the term, because one of the many names I have been called is Kiriel. It's my favorite, from a language no longer in use, no longer remembered, and its meaning is "mirror of souls."

My function has always been to echo souls' regrets back at them, thus letting them feel the full burden of their shame, guilt, and sorrow. These emotions, in order to be fully experienced, also require the sufferer to know that the sins which caused them are no longer secret, but have been witnessed.

By acting as echo, I become that witness.

Now, in Shaun's body, I didn't have to be a mirror anymore. I got to cast my *own* reflection. To be cause instead of effect.

And for the first time, I was faced with *sleep*.

I know a little about dreams, but only secondhand, and sleep itself has always been a complete mystery. The soul doesn't leave the body, but it doesn't need sleep the way a body does. And what happens to the soul during sleep, I haven't been able to tell.

I said good-night to Shaun's mother and brother, and from their rooms I heard the soft tread of feet on the floor, the clicking of light switches, the squeaking of bed-springs.

I did not turn out the lights in Shaun's room. I stayed up, looking through his drawers, through his closet, wanting to see and touch and smell and taste all I could.

I knew my time here was limited. I was surprised I'd been allowed to linger so long already. I was out of my sphere, out of my designated place in the scheme of the universe. What I was doing wasn't allowed.

I'd be forced to go back, and sooner rather than later. What more natural time to be kicked out of this existence than when Shaun's body was asleep and I was unaware?

Down the hall, I heard Jason cough.

From Shaun's mom's room, only silence.

I wasn't ready to lose my grip on this earthly plane. I wouldn't sleep till I had to.

I found a box containing Shaun's old rock collection

and pulled each rock out, examining it. I couldn't detect any smell, and the few I popped into Shaun's mouth and rolled around on his tongue had no taste at all. But each one was quite different from the others in color, texture, and weight.

As I looked and felt, Shaun's eyelids grew heavy. His body needed to shut down, to recharge.

I forced the eyelids open wide. I put the box back in Shaun's closet and sat on his bed, looking at some of his magazines. He didn't have many. An old *Sports Illustrated* with flawless women in scanty clothing, cavorting on beaches. A catalogue of sporting equipment and clothes.

My mind grew fuzzier and fuzzier, as if melting from the edges in. This was sleepiness, no question—a dullness that begged the mind to go blank.

I found myself staring at the catalogue, not seeing the page.

It occurred to me: maybe I *wouldn't* go back to my function when Shaun's body slept.

Maybe I wouldn't be allowed to.

When sleep overtook this body, would I *die*, as Shaun had? I'd done that which shouldn't be done. Would I now end up in my own domain, this time undergoing the same interminable torments I'd always supervised?

Or would I disappear completely, a flame in an environment without air?

Was this human fear I felt—this dread, this reluctance to sleep even when Shaun's body was crying out to do so?

After the Rebellion, when divine judgment loomed, I was afraid. I didn't know what lay ahead. I just knew that there was no escape.

This fear was nothing, compared to that. This fear was a delicious knot taking shape inside. Yes, I was afraid of what might happen to me. But the fear was delicious because it was my *own* emotion, inside *my* mind, created by *my* actions. For me and from me.

I already lived in Hell. Anything worse than that would only be a matter of degree.

Besides, whatever happened next, I deserved it. I never felt I particularly deserved to be punished for the Rebellion. That was undertaken—for my part—with hope and expectation and a sense of justice. I wanted to do more than appreciate, exalt, and honor; I wanted to take an active hand in the creation of the cosmos, to have an influence that was all my own.

The Rebellion wasn't a physical act, because we are not physical creatures. It was a spiritual uprising, an unauthorized outpouring of zeal. Picture a huge tree, rising for yards before spreading into a magnificent canopy, with a complex network of roots that spread unseen under your feet; the whole thing replete with green shade in the summer and lacelike boughs in the winter, perfect in its complexity, changing and yet unchanging, and wondrous to watch over time.

And then, suddenly, a lone twiggy stick appears on its trunk, growing a few feet above the ground. That's what the Rebellion was. It wasn't pretty; it didn't fit in. It turned out to be a tiny, twisted, pathetic imitation of the Creator's will; it turned out to be based in mistaken audacity and pride, and the shame of it has kept all of us diligently at our wretched and paltry tasks ever since.

But at the time, it was done with goodwill.

On the other hand, I had stolen Shaun's body with a clear sense of it being wrong. I had deserted my assigned duties. Abandoned ship, so to speak.

This time, I didn't just deserve punishment. I *owned* it. I *reveled* in it. The consequences were *mine. Take that, Creator!*

With that thought, I felt I was ready to attempt sleep. Shaun's body had wanted to for some time, desperately so.

I turned out the light and made my way to Shaun's bed in the dark, shuffling carefully, hands feeling in the dark. There—a mattress, just knee-high.

I lay down on Shaun's bed and pulled the covers up. I had always pictured going to sleep as a slow fall, like being dropped bit by bit into a bottomless hole. Would it really be like that?

Now I would find out. I allowed Shaun's eyes to close,

and while I waited, I had the most delicious thought of all: perhaps I might have finally managed to elicit the attention of the Creator Himself, even if that attention was composed of wrath. Perhaps these deliberate acts of mine would prompt Him to notice me personally.

Terror and oblivion would be worth that!

*. . . and the evening and the
morning were the first day . . .*

6

When I came back to myself, the first thing I felt was gravity. It pulled my cheek down against the sheets, pressed one side of my body down into the mattress.

My cheek? *My* body?

No. *Shaun's.*

I opened Shaun's eyes.

Yes! I was still here, and Shaun's body was still wrapped around me.

What was sleep?

Nothingness.

Lost time.

Only the Creator knew what purpose it served.

I sat up. I was a little groggy, but felt great. I raised one of Shaun's hands over my head in a fist, and punched the air in victory. I wanted to shout, but thought it would be better not to alarm Shaun's family. *"Hoo! Hoo! Hoo!"* I whispered instead, trying to sound like a cheering crowd. I've always wanted to do that.

I still didn't know how much time I'd have. I lowered Shaun's arm and looked around with satisfaction. How wonderful to see a real live earthly morning! The room had changed color subtly with the morning light, the forest green paint of the walls taking on a rich, hopeful glow. It was the same room I'd gone to sleep in last night, yet ever so slightly different.

I had shut the door when I'd retired, but someone must have opened it at some point, because it was ajar and Shaun's cat was staring at me from atop the dresser.

"Good morning, Peanut," I told the cat in a friendly manner.

He stared at me, unblinking.

"It's a pleasure to be here again."

Peanut didn't move.

"There's nothing to be afraid of. I'm not going to hurt you. Would you like to come over here and be petted?" I patted the bed beside me.

Peanut laid his ears back and hissed.

He'd never treated Shaun that way. He definitely knew I wasn't Shaun.

I thought, *Perhaps he misses his owner.* For a split second,

I almost felt bad about what I'd done.

But not quite. Shaun would not have been here, whether I had taken his body or not.

And I didn't like it when Peanut leaped off the dresser and ran under the bed. I wanted to pet him.

So I lay on Shaun's stomach and pulled myself to the edge of the bed to lean over and look underneath it. I had to lift the edge of the bedspread to do so.

In the darkness were two glowing orbs. They must be Peanut's eyes—but now they had turned luminous green and gold, as if lit from within. I caught my breath.

"You're a beautiful creature," I told the unseen Peanut. "You're a lovely creation."

I reached toward him, offering my hand.

The two orbs leaped toward me, and a ripping pain opened up in Shaun's fingertips. I jerked back as Peanut darted out, a brown blur disappearing into the hall.

When I sat up on the bed, Shaun's fingertips were bleeding from thin, razorlike scratches.

It hurt like hell. So to speak.

I held the fingers up and stared at the slashes, already welling red. It was a bright, compelling color, but the slashes felt sharp and raw, as if the very air in the room was raking the bare nerve endings.

"It hurts," I heard someone say in a low voice, and then I realized it was me. I sounded puzzled, I thought.

But I knew there was another emotion in my voice as well.

The cat knew I wasn't Shaun. But maybe that wasn't why he'd rejected me. Maybe he knew *other* things that humans didn't.

Perhaps he, an animal, sensed that I was *supposed* to be rejected. Perhaps this animal was nearer to the Creator's heart than humans were, and as such was *made* to be closed to the Fallen.

Perhaps he was a reflection of the *Creator's* rejection.

It is no small thing to be shut off from the one thing you long to know more than any other.

The blood slowly formed small blobs. Then gravity took over and it turned into drops, sliding slowly down Shaun's fingers.

Why would an all-knowing One create a being and give it a nature—give it desire, give it need—and then reject that being for doing what its nature called it to do? Why would He insert imperfections into His creations and then punish them for not being able to overcome those imperfections?

If you're one of the imperfect, you don't know the answer. And you'll never be given it.

No matter how many times you ask.

7

"Good morning, Jason," I said as I came into the kitchen.

"Bite me, Shaun," said Jason.

Jason may not like Shaun at all, but I really like Jason. He doesn't know it, but he has a lot in common with the Fallen. From the time he was small, Jason has been disliked and rejected because of his nature. He was always very active, unable to sit still. Whenever he saw something that interested him, he had to touch it, take it in his hands. And then he couldn't just look at it; he had to work it, move it, bend it until it broke. His babysitters and teachers used to tighten with dread when they saw him coming, and when they corrected him, their words were angry and impatient.

If I was aware of their reactions, you can bet Jason was, too.

Oddly enough, bending things till they break is a trait that Jason has in common with the Boss; it is also the Boss's nature to want to test the limits of things. And like Jason, he doesn't do it out of disregard for the feelings or property of others, but out of irrepressible curiosity.

The Boss is still irrepressible. Jason is not. All the years of being dreaded, of being punished and disliked because of his actions, have made Jason retreat into a fortress of cynical loathing. It's there in his surliness for anyone to see. Not that anyone cares to try much.

I feel a kinship with the Jasons of the world. So although I did not speak to him, I fixed myself a Shaunian breakfast of Froot Loops with milk, then pulled out a chair and sat at the kitchen table with my new brother. I liked being in the same room with him.

He downed his Cinnamon Toast Crunch while I poked Froot Loops with my spoon and watched them disappear under the milk, then bob back up.

They tasted even better than ketchup.

Jason finished his breakfast and rose to leave. I spoke to him kindly.

"Have a good day, Jason," I told him as he picked up his backpack and slung it over his shoulder.

"Get bent, Shaun," Jason answered without looking around. He strode out of the kitchen, and a moment later I heard the front door open and shut.

He didn't brush his teeth, I thought. I had, last night—had rubbed the tiny little brush in circles against each tiny little tooth. I would do so again in a moment.

The Froot Loops had been crunchy at first; now they were soggy. Still good, though; I chased the last ones around and captured them with my spoon. Then I lifted the bowl to Shaun's lips and drank the last of the milk. It was sweet and tasty.

I completed Shaun's morning routine except for a few minor changes. Shaun always leaves his bowl and spoon in the sink, but I put them in the dishwasher to save Shaun's mom some time later. And I flossed; Shaun almost never does that.

I grabbed Shaun's backpack out of his room and was headed through the living room when a speck of white caught my eye. A piece of notebook paper, on the coffee table.

Jason's homework. It was wrinkled and covered with writing: messy, heavily scrawled pencil marks with many erasures. One had even torn through the paper.

He'd forgotten to take it.

I thought of the way he'd looked, hunched over his work; the way his hair had been sticking up last night. He'd labored over this page. Yet at school today, it would be as if he hadn't done it at all.

There was nothing I could do about it. Jason's bus

would already have left. I still had to catch Shaun's.

I pushed away a twinge of sympathy. This was my holiday, my vacation, away from the sorrow and pain of others. I had been saturated with all that for most of my miserable existence. Those feelings were exactly what I was trying to get away from.

This holiday was about having *fun*.

I set the paper back on the coffee table and left, locking the front door behind me.

8

I thought, as I headed out to catch Shaun's school bus, that I wanted to eat some cookies today. Maybe chocolate would be best. To start with, anyway.

I wore Shaun's headphones while I waited for the bus, listening to one of his CDs. The music reminded me of his messy room; the noises piled and draped over one another so that I couldn't distinguish them. I didn't like the way the CD drowned out all other sounds, anyway, so I took the headphones off and put the player in his backpack.

Shaun always seemed embarrassed, standing by himself on this corner, waiting all alone. He stuck his hands in his pockets and wouldn't look up when anyone drove by. It was as if he felt vulnerable.

I didn't quite understand why. I don't know what terrible thing he thought might happen if people saw him alone.

I *liked* standing alone.

I looked around at the way the wind blew the leaves on the trees. I imagined this must be the way a school of fish looked, each one moving separately but in unison, each maintaining its own space.

I watched one squirrel chasing another in the yard across the street; at first it looked like they were playing, but after some observation I decided it was a territorial dispute and that one was trying to bite the other's balls off.

Then I closed Shaun's eyes and listened to myself hum; I liked the way it made the inside of Shaun's head vibrate. It also sounded different when I stuck my fingers in Shaun's ears—much louder.

So I did not hear the bus, but I smelled the gasoline fumes—slightly unpleasant, compared to the fresh morning smell of damp grass. When I opened Shaun's eyes, several faces were staring at me through the open bus windows, some puzzled, others leering.

I removed Shaun's fingers from his ears and climbed the bus steps. "Good morning," I said to the bus driver, who nodded at me with a slight grin.

I went to sit next to Bailey, which is what Shaun

always did. "What were you *doing* out there?" Bailey asked as I slid into the seat.

"Nothing," I said. That was Shaun's stock answer; I felt it should be mine, too.

Bailey eyed my collared shirt and khakis. "What's up with the clothes?"

"Um. Everything else is dirty," I lied. I didn't want to get into a discussion about fashion right now. It was my first time to ride in a motor vehicle, and I didn't want to miss anything.

Interesting—after the initial start, which threw me back against the seat, all I could feel was a humming vibration under me. I peered around Bailey and out the window. If I hadn't seen the houses and trees going by, I might not have known I was moving at—what? Twenty, thirty miles an hour?

Fascinating.

"How come you weren't online last night?" Bailey was asking.

"I didn't have time." That was true. "Can I sit by the window?"

He gave me another odd look—I couldn't interpret this one—then shrugged and stood up. I scooted over while he pressed himself against the seat in front of us.

"Hey! Sit down back there!"

That was the bus driver. All I could see was the back

of her head. Then I saw the mirror above her. Her face was reflected in it, and she appeared to be glaring at me.

Even though she was facing the opposite direction, we could see each other. How clever.

The window was open, and I stuck Shaun's hand out of it to see if I could feel the air as we passed.

Yes, I could. A cool, rushing pressure.

"Hey!" shouted the bus driver. "You!" I looked up at the rearview mirror; she was glaring at me again. "Do you want to *walk*? Get that hand back in this bus!"

I pulled Shaun's hand back in. But I wanted to understand. "Why?" I asked the bus driver.

In the mirror, she seemed to expand, to swell till she filled the whole frame. "*Why*? Are you asking me *why*?"

I started to say yes, but she didn't wait for an answer.

"Because I *said* so," she thundered. "*That's* why!"

Being in Shaun was in some ways like being shut up in a box. Before, I had no sight, but I was *aware* of everything. Now I *saw*, and what I saw was only the driver's back, and her eyes in a mirror.

I felt sure that she was angry, though.

I remembered that she always went on about people following the rules. Apparently she liked her job to be uneventful; perhaps it was stressful to her when students on her bus or other cars on the road did anything different from what they did on every other day.

Like sticking a hand out of the window, apparently.

So I said nothing, but kept my hand away from the window for the rest of the ride.

9

I knew what Shaun's mother believed about Shaun's love interest. A while back, she'd found a note from a girl in one of his pockets. She put it back and never told Shaun she found it, I suppose because she feared he'd think she'd been snooping. Although she had been.

The note wasn't what she thought; it was from a girl that Shaun liked—or rather, lusted for. The note wasn't even written to him. It had fallen on the floor, and he'd picked it up on the way out of class. He had actually masturbated over it once before becoming ashamed. I knew he was ashamed because of what he said afterward. "You pervert," he'd whispered to himself in the mirror.

Even so, he didn't throw the note away. He took it out every once in a while and looked at it, smoothing the

paper with his fingers.

I wish I'd known what he was thinking then.

For Shaun, this was all much easier than actually speaking to the girl, which indeed would have been a mistake, because not only had she shown no interest in him, she almost certainly didn't know who he was. Shaun was not bad-looking, but in the hierarchy of twenty-first-century American high schools, looks don't always matter as much as self-confidence. And except in the presence of his closest friends, Shaun slunk around hunched in on himself, speaking only when spoken to, and that in uncommunicative monosyllables.

Thus, he was mostly invisible.

The girl who wrote the note, who apparently occupied much of his thoughts, was generally spoken of as being quite attractive, compared to the rest of his classmates. Specifically, it seemed she had largish breasts, a small waist, slender legs, and facial features that were pleasingly symmetrical.

I didn't care about these things. It was the *feeling* I wanted, the feeling my—or Shaun's—body would have while engaging in the sexual act. It didn't matter with whom the act occurred so long as I experienced my side of it.

With this in mind, I knew a better candidate than anyone Shaun would have chosen.

Her name was Lane. Lane Henneberger. She'd had a crush on Shaun for some time. She wrote things like "Mrs. Shaun Simmons" in her diary, which she kept locked and hidden under her mattress. According to her writings, she also worried that she was the only virgin left in her high school—although she wasn't, not by far—and she'd had vague dreams of Shaun letting her know that he'd secretly been in love with her for some time. After which exchange of information they'd make tender love and Lane would lose her dreaded virginity, thus making her—or so she imagined—like all the other girls who were wanted and desired.

Shaun, of course, never noticed anything out of the ordinary about Lane. I felt sure that if he'd thought about her at all, he would have been critical of her wide hips, flat chest, and large nose.

Shaun never was the sharpest tool in the shed.

10

Shaun's first class was World History. I already knew everything about World History, so I decided to spend my time thinking about Lane Henneberger instead.

As the teacher talked about ancient Rome, I came to the realization that Shaun couldn't just go up to Lane and ask her to have intercourse. A lot of human beings—females in particular—frown upon that.

Hmm. This might be a problem. I didn't want to spend a lot of time on achieving a sexual experience. Didn't want to build a relationship, especially not one built on trust. I didn't want to hurt anyone, because I didn't want to be around any more hurt.

So far, I felt I *hadn't* hurt anyone. I'd had no more impact—negative *or* positive—than I did in my regular job.

Now I just wanted to have a go at sex in Shaun's body without creating any bad feelings whatsoever.

Perhaps Lane wasn't the best option after all?

I thought again about the large-breasted girl Shaun liked.

No. Unfortunately for Shaun's taste, she just wasn't an acceptable candidate. Even if I was wrong and she did know who Shaun was, I felt sure she would think him beneath her. I remembered her comments about people who didn't have her commitment to fashion.

Really, there weren't many options at all, not for Shaun. A few girls at school seemed sexually adventurous. I knew who they were. But they didn't know Shaun, and I wasn't sure they'd want him if they did; he certainly hadn't been very attractive to females thus far.

In this body, I did not have access to prostitutes. Rape was not a consideration.

No, Lane Henneberger would have to do.

With a start, I realized that the teacher was calling Shaun's name.

"Would you like to join us?" she asked.

"Sure," I said. "In what?"

The class laughed.

"In paying attention."

"Oh. Of course. Sorry," I added, thinking that now would not be a good time to point out that the notes on

the board behind her were wrong, that the emperor Nero did *not* order the burning of Rome; apparently the teacher had been reading Suetonius, who had many axes to grind when he wrote his histories.

When the bell rang, I tucked Shaun's books under his arm and headed into the hall. Really, this place wasn't conducive to learning. It was a factory designed to get the most products through the assembly line with as little trouble as possible. A product that wouldn't quite fit through the premanufactured machinery—a product like, say, Jason—was doomed to be chewed up and spit out.

The primary lesson in this place, I thought, is to move according to the sound of bells, to sit still, and to be quiet. And if you can't do all three of those, you're going to be considered a failure in one way or another.

This is what I was thinking when I saw Lane.

I saw her and immediately was hit with a flood of Lust.

The human mind is an odd, flexible, vivid thing; I had never *seen* Lane, not through physical eyes, but now I immediately imagined her naked. I pictured her ample hips, her small breasts that had never been touched by anyone except herself, her willingness to be splayed in various positions by Shaun.

If she really knew Shaun, I thought, she might not like

him very much. He didn't seem to have much to recommend him.

But I liked *her*, tremendously. I liked the way she treated her family—unlike the way Shaun treated his. I liked her interest in the things she learned in class. I liked the way she tried new foods in ethnic restaurants.

Now, looking at Lane Henneberger walking down the hall with her books clutched in her arms, I wondered if I was experiencing love.

From the human standpoint, it often starts like this: with a chemical attraction, a physical reaction of the body's hormones. Sometimes it smoothes out into an attraction of mind and soul. Sometimes the attraction fades, but that doesn't necessarily mean the love itself was never there. Each case is different.

In this case, I knew Lane, I liked her immensely, and I was fascinated with her color, her shape, and her textures, as well as the nuances of her body's movements and what they might say about her thoughts and feelings.

I followed her down the hall. Sometimes, when she was close enough, I thought I caught the faint scent of perfume. Then we'd be separated in the crowd and I'd have to jostle to catch up. Once I walked right behind her, close enough that if I'd leaned forward, I could have touched Shaun's lips to her hair. It was beautiful, even Shaun would have to admit that—long, a color that I imagined compared to toffee or honey, soft and luscious looking. I wanted to wrap it around my fingers, feel it against my nose and lips, nuzzle it aside to sniff her bare flesh.

By this time Shaun's body was showing the effects of my thoughts, and, as Shaun did, I held his books in front of him. And kept walking behind Lane.

I am in love, I decided.

Her hair was so bewitching, I reached out a hand to touch it—just one finger—and oh, it was as glossy-smooth and soft as it looked.

At my touch, Lane stopped and whirled around. Her eyes were wide—perhaps with fear?—but the moment she saw who it was, her lovely face softened.

Shaun, you idiot—were you blind?

"What were you just doing?" she asked.

"You've got beautiful hair," I told her. Her eyes were beautiful, too—a light brown. She blinked, surprised, and her lashes swept her cheeks.

"Thanks" was all she said. But a quick smile slipped out before she hid it, and I felt Shaun's heart give a little throb in his chest.

I could not think of a thing to say.

"Well," Lane Henneberger said, "I guess I'd better get to class."

I wanted to say, *No, let's leave school and go outside to*

make love on the grass. But I managed just to nod. *Whatever you desire, my sweet.*

But when she started walking again, I found that I was walking beside her. We stayed side by side in silence down the entire length of the hall.

"Why are you walking with me?" she asked as we turned the corner together.

"Because I want to," I told her. "Do you mind?"

She shook her head, and neither of us said anything all the way to her science classroom.

At the door, she slowed and then stopped, as if unsure whether to go in.

Finally, she turned to face me. "You're different today." I watched her lips part and move, and pictured them slightly damp, sliding over various parts of Shaun's body. "I mean, besides talking to me and all." Her words came out fast, uneven, and I wondered if she was nervous. "Which I mean, you know, you never really do. Talk to me. But aside from that, you seem, um, different."

I stopped watching her lips and focused on her eyes. "How so?"

"Well . . . for one thing, you're smiling. You hardly ever smile."

Was I smiling? I put Shaun's fingertips up to feel his face. Yes, there were certainly teeth revealed, and Shaun's cheeks were pushed higher than usual by muscular contractions. "It's because I'm happy," I explained to Lane.

"You're really cute when you smile," she said. Almost before the words were out, her face turned a lovely pinkish shade, and she ducked her head and fled into the classroom.

She would know if I was different. She watched Shaun all the time.

Lane Henneberger, I thought, *you are no fool.*

11

Bailey and I went to lunch together after Computer Applications. I heard him talking about his PowerPoint presentation, but I was thinking about Lane, who had geometry this period.

"You all right?" Bailey asked as we got in line.

"Yes."

"You're acting kind of weird today."

"I'm in love," I told him.

Bailey snorted. "Oh yeah? Who with?"

"Lane Henneberger."

A laugh that sounded like a bark burst out of him. "O-*kay*," he said, shaking his head. "Whatever. Looks like pizza today," he said, standing on tiptoes to see over the shoulders of the people in front of him. "Pepperoni," he added.

I shut my eyes to see if I could bring the scent of Lane's perfume back into my head. No, not quite. But it made me happy to think of it.

When I opened my eyes again, Bailey was staring at me.

"You're not serious, are you?" he asked.

"I'm very serious."

"You can't be."

"I am. I love her."

"Dude," Bailey said, and he wasn't smiling at all now. "She's a *dog*."

"Not at all. You're blinded by the prejudices of this tiny little society called high school. She's quite attractive."

"She's *fat*."

"As I said—uh, like I said, dude. You're prejudiced."

"You've gone off the deep end."

"The only deep end that I'm going off is Lane Henneberger's."

"You mean . . ." The line shifted around us, but Bailey didn't move; he eyed me as if he was trying to figure something out. "What *do* you mean?"

"I'm going to plunge myself into the expanses of her many charms. The line's moving, Bailey; scoot up."

Bailey scooted up. Then he turned back to me. "You're

saying . . . you mean . . . you're going to *do* her?"

"That's one way to put it."

Human eyes are amazing. Bailey was looking at me, but something about his expression was far away, and I felt sure—just from visual observation!—that he was working this out in his head, perhaps weighing the idea of sex with Lane against his only fulfillment of lust, which involved manga comics and a bottle of lotion. He had been caught off guard, I could tell. But now it seemed to me that he was rethinking. Considering.

Finally he focused on me. "Dude!" he said with a grin. He held his hand up, palm toward me.

I knew he had accepted and approved of my quest, and wanted me to slap his hand.

So I did.

"You know she lives up the street from me," said Bailey.

"I know." I looked down at the steel bars that lay like a flat shelf along the front of the food line. Their burnished gleam seemed to beckon to me. The net-headed ladies behind the counter would soon give me a food-filled tray, and I'd get to slide it along that shining length.

Only it turned out to be not as much fun as I thought. I was hemmed in by Bailey in front and another boy behind, and could only slide my tray in short spurts. I wanted to give it a shove and see how far it would go.

I stopped and let Bailey go on ahead.

"Move," said the boy behind me, but I waited till Bailey was far down the line, reaching for a small bottle of chocolate milk. I didn't want his hand to get pinched if my tray did make it that far.

I eyed the distance. Put a hand on each side of the tray. Pulled it back, and . . .

Whoosh! One shove sent the tray flying down the silver rails.

"Hey!" said one of the net-headed ladies. "None of that!"

The tray slid to a stop as Bailey set his milk down. He moved on without even looking around.

"Having fun?" the boy next to me drawled. He didn't seem to want an answer, though, because he turned to talk to another boy behind him.

I paid for Shaun's meal, followed Bailey to a table—he and Shaun always sat in the same place—and set to work eating.

The pizza was not quite what I expected. Chewy. "Rubbery" might have been the word. Next to it were some whitish bulbous things in a clear sauce or juice; when I bit into them, they were soft yet grainy.

"What are these?" I asked Bailey. "Potatoes?"

"Pears, duh."

"I think I like them."

"That's good to hear, dude. I'm so glad you told me. Hey, my mom got me Tectonic Warriors 2 last night. We can try it out after school."

"Okay." As I tried to get a fork into my slippery second pear, a thought hit me. "Hey. Maybe Jason could come, too."

"Jason who?"

"Jason, my little brother."

"Oh. Right." Bailey stuffed the last of the pizza into his mouth. "Are you, like, babysitting or something?"

I shook my head. "Jason's too old to be babysat. It's just that he's pretty good at Tectonic Warriors. The first one, anyway."

"Okay. Whatever."

"Are you going to eat your pears?"

"Doubt it."

"Can I have them?"

He pushed his tray at me. "They're all yours."

"Thanks." I stabbed them and transported them, dripping, to my own tray.

When we were finished eating, we carried the trays over to a window cut into the wall between the cafeteria and the kitchen. They certainly had an efficient system set up; I dumped the leftover liquid and ice from my cup into a large garbage can with a screen over it, threw the used paper goods into another can, and then put the tray itself on a stainless steel counter.

"Silverware in the tub," growled a different lady with a net. They all wore white and had nets, but their sizes and shapes and faces were different.

I pulled my tray back and, removing the fork and knife, placed them carefully in a rectangular container filled with soapy water. Then I pushed the tray forward again. Then I waited, but this particular net-headed lady did not say thank you.

Bailey now attempted to drop his silverware in the water, but before he could do so, another boy shouldered him aside. "Move it," the boy said as Bailey shuffled to keep his balance.

The boy who had shoved Bailey dumped his tray and moved away. Bailey ignored the whole incident and went about his business.

I watched the other boy walk over to a group of his friends. He was one of those sowers of pain, as I thought of them: the type who plant fear, self-doubt, and self-loathing into others who aren't strong enough to resist. Some sowers of pain do it on purpose, but most do it thoughtlessly, as a matter of course.

I'd seen thousands, millions, of these beings. I'd spent too many depressing eons with them after they were dead. After they were weighed down with guilt over the hurt they'd caused others.

So *this* was what they were like in person. Sandy hair. A few pimples. Many of the men and teenage boys I'd seen so far seemed to have broad shoulders and a body that tapered downward, like a carrot, but this sower of pain—his name was Reed McGowan—was shaped rather like a can of soda.

I knew Reed had his own troubles. Insecurity piled upon insecurity. I knew I should feel sorry for him.

But just looking at him made me tired. People like Reed spent eternity torturing themselves—torturing *me*—because they were too thick to take control of their behavior when they'd had the chance.

I was watching him when it hit me.

Here, in this physical body, I might *finally* be able to have an impact on one of these types.

Face-to-face with him while he's still in the flesh! And me with the ability to access spoken language!

Yes, with a well-chosen word or two, I just might be able to save us both some suffering in the eons to come.

"Hey!" I called. "Reed McGowan."

He looked around.

"Tend to your own life," I told him. "And—word of advice—you'll do better in the long run if you start trying to appreciate what's all around you rather than picking it apart."

Reed's mouth hung open rather unattractively. Then

he shut it. *"What?"* he said.

All his friends had turned and were staring at me. "Believe me," I told him, "later you'll be sorry that you spent so much time tearing other people down."

Then I realized I wasn't talking like Shaun.

"Or whatever," I added, and turned away.

Bailey and Shaun always went outside after lunch. As we headed across the cafeteria together, I saw a look on Bailey's face that I thought I could interpret.

Are you crazy? it said.

He didn't say anything, though, just accompanied me through the door and outside, where groups of students were clustered.

"Next time you want to commit suicide," he mentioned as we stepped off the concrete steps onto the asphalt, "please don't do it when I'm with—"

I felt a hand on my shoulder.

"Hey, asswipe," Reed said as he spun me around to face him.

I knew his modus operandi, as they say. He had followed me out here where there was less supervision. Where he had more of a chance to be physically intimidating.

What a waste of his time and energy.

Continue to be patient with him, I told myself. *Be understanding. There's fright behind his meanness.*

Most of his insecurities were petty and normal. But there was one in particular I thought I could help with.

"There's no need to be afraid," I told him, trying to keep my voice low. I knew this wouldn't be something he'd want others to hear.

"Oh yeah?" He laughed—no, actually it was something halfway between a laugh and a sneer. "What do you think I'm afraid of? You?"

"No," I told him, still very low. "You're afraid that you have a small penis."

Bailey heard. His eyes grew so wide, the whites of them showed.

Reed's face had gone pale.

But I *knew* him. I knew he measured himself over and over with a ruler, knew that he searched the Internet for information on penis size, looking at porn not for sexual but for comparative purposes.

"Actually," I tried to assure him, "there's nothing to fear. Your penis may be shorter than most when it's flaccid, but when it's erect, it's well within the average range. So there's no need for this blustering—"

That's when Reed's fist smashed into me.

12

"You're lucky he only hit you once," Bailey said on the bus ride home that afternoon.

"Once was plenty," I agreed.

"I think it's because you stayed down. That was a smart move. Good thinking, dude."

"Yeah." I hadn't stayed down because it was a smart move, or because I'd been thinking at all. I'd stayed down because it *hurt*.

It's been said that emotional pain is worse than physical pain, and I will agree that in general it lasts longer. But the moment when Reed hit me was much sharper than anything I'd felt before. If interminable emotional pain could be compressed into a split-second flash, I thought, it would end up feeling an awful lot like Reed

McGowan's right hook.

I didn't know why I'd even bothered. Why should *I* be able to turn him away from his self-chosen path? Instruction has never been part of my function. I don't get to teach. I don't get to influence. I don't get to affect.

What I get to do is receive and reflect.

I wasn't reflecting now, I was absorbing. I could no longer call this face *Shaun's*. The raw, throbbing pain in Shaun's left jaw was *mine*. The nerve endings were *mine*. The swollen lip was *mine*.

This body was *mine*.

I had to admit, though, that the problem with my encounter with Reed was that I hadn't acted enough like Shaun. That's what I was supposed to be doing: quietly acting like Shaun. I was lucky I hadn't attracted the attention of the higher-ups yet.

The more disruptions I caused, the sooner I'd be dragged out of here.

I'd have to be more careful. Try to stretch this puppy out as long as I could.

"You going to get off with me?" Bailey asked.

It took me a moment to fill the blanks in his question. What he'd really meant to ask was, *We are half a block from my bus stop. Do you still want to come to my house after school to play video games, and if so, do you need to go by your house first to take care of something and then walk to my house after-*

ward, or can you exit the bus with me and walk straight to my house?

"I gotta go home and see if Jason wants to come," I told Bailey.

"Oh, yeah."

I hadn't thought much of Bailey before—he hadn't seemed to warrant much thought—but now I was beginning to like him. After an initial knee-jerk negative reaction, he'd been willing to try seeing Lane Henneberger from a new point of view. He hadn't been angry when Reed shoved him. Now he didn't seem to care one way or the other if Jason joined us. He certainly was an easygoing fellow. He seemed to accept whatever was set in front of him with good humor.

And Shaun, I thought, could easily have included Jason in his activities before this.

The bus squealed to a stop, pressing my back against the seat.

"See you in a bit." Bailey stood up and made his way to the front, then disappeared down the steps. He didn't look back or wave, although I watched. He just assumed Shaun was there, and would always be there.

Humans take so much for granted.

At my stop, I decided to try running home. As soon as the bus departed I increased my pace, walking faster and faster, until it felt natural to break into what might be

called a jog. My backpack jounced uncomfortably and my breath came harder and faster, but I sped up anyway, stretching and pumping my leg muscles to their limits, to see how it felt.

It felt good.

For about ten seconds. Then my lungs couldn't get enough air. It was as if a boulder had arisen in my chest. My legs slowed of their own accord, and my breath came in gasps.

I hadn't noticed how *sweet* air was. It rushed into my body the way I imagined water would flood into a desert.

When I walked into the house, Jason's backpack was on the floor next to the front door. The paper he'd forgotten was still on the coffee table. Jason himself must be in the kitchen; I heard rummaging sounds from there.

I picked up his forgotten assignment and walked into the kitchen, to find Jason standing at the counter, ripping open a bag that said "Chips Ahoy!"

Cookies!

"You left this here this morning," I said, holding the paper out.

Jason looked around, stuffing a cookie into his mouth. He seemed a little puzzled at the sight of his assignment, but took it with a shrug. "Fanks," he said through his cookie.

A sweet scent wafted out of the open cookie bag.

"Rich Chocolate Chips In Every Bite!" it said, in red print.

"Can I have one?" I asked Jason.

"No."

Mistake: Shaun would never have asked. He would have taken it without asking, even if he had to put Jason in a headlock.

I didn't want to put Jason in a headlock, but I *really* wanted a cookie.

"What happened to your lip?" Jason asked while I was thinking it over.

"Nothing." I darted a hand out and got hold of the bag. Jason pulled it away, but a few cookies fell out onto the counter. I picked one up and took a bite as Jason retreated around the kitchen island with the bag.

Ohhh. Good. Crunchy at first. And then little bits melting on my tongue.

"Bailey's got Tectonic Warriors 2," I told Jason, "and I'm going over there in a minute to play. You want to come?"

At the words "Tectonic Warriors 2," Jason's eyes fastened on me. Then they narrowed. "Why?" he asked.

"Because it's fun."

"No kidding. Why are you asking *me*?"

"Because I thought you'd like it."

Several emotions flickered across Jason's face, so

quickly that I couldn't follow them.

"No thanks, dickhead," he finally said. He let scorn drip through his voice.

I picked up another cookie and took a bite. This time I didn't chew, but let my saliva dissolve it.

Not as much fun, I decided. Chewing was better.

I just needed to be careful chewing. My lower lip was a bit sore.

Jason was watching me from the other side of the kitchen. "You fall down or something?"

I thought about it. Shaun would have told him to shut up, or to mind his own freaking business.

"Reed McGowan hit me," I told Jason.

"Reed McGowan? The guy who used to punch brick walls for money?"

"Yes."

Jason shook his head. "Idiot."

"Me or Reed McGowan?"

"*You!* What a moron! Were you *fighting* him?"

"No. I just made him mad."

Jason rummaged in the bag and pulled out another cookie. I finished my own cookie and reached for the last one lying on the counter.

"How did you make him mad?" Jason asked.

"I think the thing that set him off was when I told him he had a small penis."

Jason's laugh was harsh, almost rusty, as if he didn't use it very often. "You told *Reed McGowan* he had a tiny dick?"

"No. A small penis."

"God. I can't believe he even let you live. Why'd you say that?"

I shrugged.

"You're crazy," Jason said, shaking his head again. But he was smiling. I couldn't quite follow his emotions. "Here. *You* put 'em up." He tossed the bag onto the counter and headed out to the living room.

I took out six cookies, slipped them into my shirt pocket, then rolled the cookie bag shut and sealed it. As I was putting it back into the cabinet, I saw that Jason had left his late homework paper on the island.

I picked it up and took it into the living room.

Jason wasn't there. I stood in the middle of the floor. Where could he have gone? He always came in, got a snack, and sat in front of the TV.

A faint whirring sound came from down the hall.

The bathroom fan. He was in the bathroom.

I started to set his paper down on the coffee table. But he'd already forgotten it there once, and then again on the kitchen counter; it seemed unlikely he'd remember it this third time.

I unzipped his backpack, looking amidst wadded

papers and books with scribbled-on covers for a folder to put the paper in. There it was, worn and coming apart at the seams: ENGLISH.

I pulled it out, put Jason's paper in one of the pockets, and stuffed the folder into the backpack. Then I zipped the backpack and put it on the floor again, right where Jason had left it.

Jason came out of the bathroom as I was heading down the hall to Shaun's room.

"Hey," Jason said as he passed. "I guess I might go with you to Bailey's."

This pleased me, but I didn't say anything. Shaun wouldn't have, and I had a grim feeling that I was still pushing the limits of Shaun's behavior in several ways.

I put Shaun's backpack in his room, and when I came out, Jason was sitting on the couch. The living room seemed different, somehow. I looked around, trying to figure it out.

The television wasn't on. Without it, there was no noise, no flashes of movement. Just Jason, sitting silent, waiting.

His hands were on his knees. He cast a glance at me, but didn't get up.

"Ready?" I asked him.

Jason nodded once, quickly, and stood, his mouth clamped shut.

He came hesitantly over as I opened the front door. "Are you nervous?" I asked.

"No," Jason said, in that dripping-with-scorn voice. But he didn't say anything else. And I thought he might be lying.

It really wasn't like Shaun to socialize with Jason. I supposed Jason might be worried it was some kind of trick.

"Don't worry," I told him, "we're just going to play video games."

He threw another one of those glances my way. He didn't say anything, not the whole way to Bailey's house, but I noticed that he kept several feet away from me the entire time. Just out of arm's reach. And when I stood on Bailey's front porch ringing the doorbell, he hung back on the sidewalk and didn't greet Mrs. Darnell, Bailey's mother, when she let us in.

He didn't seem to relax until we were all on the floor in Bailey's room, controllers in hand. And soon, his body was rigid with concentration, his thumbs and fingers the only things moving.

Shaun would have been delighted to play this game, but I couldn't get very interested. The buttons were pretty colors, and it was mildly amusing to see what movements they produced on the screen, but I enjoyed looking around Bailey's room more. It wasn't like Shaun's room.

Bailey had a set of shelves crammed with books, many of the same color, with numbers on their spines. On the walls were advertisements for video games and posters of large-eyed cartoon characters bearing swords and various other weapons. In the corner, a guitar stood connected to an amplifier—but unlike Shaun's guitar, Bailey's wasn't dusty; he played it fairly often. His room was much neater than Shaun's, too; no clothes lay on the floor, and his bed was made.

Still, I pushed buttons and tried to pay attention to the game. As Shaun would have done.

"Game. Over," a voice intoned from the direction of the television. I set my controller down. Bailey set his down too, and stretched. Jason remained in a battle-ready position.

"Not bad, Jason." Bailey said it in a matter-of-fact voice as he watched statistics flash onto the screen. "But Shaun," he added in the same offhanded, not unfriendly tone, "you totally suck."

"Ah well," I said. "I shall have to live with the pain." I stretched out on my back. Bailey's carpet was very soft, and thick, too, under my bare arms and hands. I thought I'd like to lie on it naked sometime, although I knew that was unlikely to come about.

Instead, I moved my arms, sliding them in a flapping motion along the carpet. Then I moved my legs, too, together and apart like scissors. "Look, I'm making a carpet angel," I said. "An *angel*, ha!" I couldn't help but chuckle. I'd made a joke. A funny one, too.

Bailey just shook his head. "It's time to pick your guy, Shaun."

"You and Jason play for a while. I want to look at some of your books."

"I thought you hated manga."

Shaun hated manga. But *I* wanted to look at it through physical eyes. The garish colors attracted me.

"I'll play in a minute," I told Bailey, and while he and Jason began another game, I got up to peruse Bailey's shelves.

The books appeared to be perfectly arranged into series, but closer inspection revealed that a very few of the numbers in some of the series were out of order. The same books also tended to have a cracked and disheveled appearance along their spines. This, I thought, revealed which books Bailey read the most, and therefore liked best.

I pulled out one of the worn books and started flipping through. It was interesting to *see* the varying strokes of the pen. A thick, solid line here evoked a slightly different emotional response than a thin and jittery line there. The girls on the pages reminded me of the flawless women in Shaun's sports magazine, except that these had impossibly long legs, and very large round eyes and heads.

I put the book back and let my eyes and fingers explore other items on Bailey's shelves. He had a coconut crudely carved into the shape of a face, with another piece of coconut tied on top for a lid. It was hairy and rough. Burned into the side of the face were the words SCHLITTERBAHN WATERPARK. The inside was hollow, containing many coins, plus a few bills of various denominations. I sniffed it. It smelled sweetly musty.

Hanging from a corner of the shelves was a fat bunch of beaded necklaces, each strand either purple, gold, or green, all glittery. I reached to touch them, and the second I felt the beads slide through my fingers, I was hooked. They swam and flowed and clicked and rattled—like clouds, like water, like . . . something. I couldn't figure out what was so satisfying about caressing them, but caress them I did. Then I stepped closer to rub them against my face. That didn't feel the same as when my hands touched them. Against my face, they felt . . . nubbly.

I realized that I was being very un-Shaun-like, and gave a guilty glance around.

Jason and Bailey were still actively engaged with their game.

Reluctantly, I let the beads fall—slowly, through my

fingers—to hang silent and still, and moved on to look at other things.

On another shelf was a stack of photographs. The top one was of Bailey leaning over a table that had a cake on it. He appeared to be blowing out the candles that stood on the cake. His latest birthday, I realized.

I lifted the top photo. The one underneath showed Bailey, apparently within moments after the last picture. This one, however, was taken from a slightly different angle that showed Shaun sitting next to him.

Shaun wasn't doing anything much. He wasn't even looking at the camera, just sitting there, leaned back in his chair. He wore a faint smile—likely he'd been watching Bailey clown around, while waiting for a slice of cake.

I looked at the next photo. The only part of Shaun showing was one of his hands. It rested on the table, an afterthought, something that wasn't meant to be noticed.

I noticed.

I lifted my hand and looked at it. It was the same as the one in the picture. Had Shaun seen this hand the same way when he'd looked at it? What had he thought, what had he felt, that day at Bailey's?

These were memories that I didn't have. I supposed they must be somewhere in Shaun's brain, hidden within the folds of gray matter that I had acquired by squatter's right. But I didn't have the key that unlocked them.

Shaun was gone. No one else knew it, but he was no longer here.

Something rose inside me, so strange that at first I didn't recognize it, although I have experienced a duller, overriding version of it almost every moment of my existence. It lurched in my body like a jagged yet leaden rock, shot through with regret and loneliness and lost chances. I had never felt it myself, only through others.

I put the photos down and turned away. I didn't want to feel grief for the loss of Shaun. Didn't want to feel *guilt*. Of all beings, I knew how pointless it was. Shaun would have died whether I'd stepped in or not. Those last moments I took from him would have been filled with either pain or nothingness.

I went back to sit on the floor next to Jason and Bailey. I said nothing, did nothing—just watched Shaun's brother and best friend. They were happily engrossed in their game, both completely unaware that the only things left of Shaun Simmons were a few photos and an empty space.

13

"Did you have a good time?" I asked Jason later, as we were walking home.

"It was okay."

I thought this meant that he'd enjoyed himself. If he hadn't, wouldn't he have said something sarcastic? Or blunt, like "It sucked"?

I wasn't positive, though. "Do you want to do this again tomorrow?" I asked Jason, testing. It pleased me to think of his being happy.

It *really* pleased me to think that I might have influenced another being's emotions.

"I guess," he said, shrugging.

He did like it, I told myself. Even though I wasn't positive.

At the house, I decided to go do Shaun's homework. While Jason turned on the television, I went straight to Shaun's room.

As soon as I crossed the threshold, I saw that Peanut was on the bed. He sat in such a fashion that he appeared to have no paws; all four legs were tucked neatly under him. He looked like a blob with a cat's head.

I had been reaching down for Shaun's backpack, which sat just inside the doorway, but now I straightened slowly. The slashes on my fingertips still stung.

I did not speak, because I thought Peanut might not like it. And I didn't want to do anything Peanut didn't like.

I thought of the photos in Bailey's room. *Peanut* knew I was an imposter. He didn't care what motivations I had, or whether I was doing any harm. He just knew that I was a thief.

I waited a few moments, but he didn't attack.

Nor did he move to leave.

I would have liked to win him over. Would have liked to try, anyway. But the way he was staring at me—steadily, unblinking, his pupils dark slits in the pale green—well, he *blamed* me, I could tell. For going against the Creator's will. For leaving my assigned place in the universe.

It was hard to meet his little cat gaze.

Slowly, carefully, I sidled out of the room.

Peanut just watched, eyes unfathomable, the victor.

For dinner that night, Shaun's mom brought home McDonald's. I had a Quarter Pounder with cheese, fries, and a Coke. This time the ketchup didn't come in a bottle, but in foil packets, each of which had a tiny dotted line marked across the corner, and little words saying "Tear Here." After tearing, I had to turn the packet upside down and squeeze to get the ketchup to come out.

I found that if I squeezed too hard—or if the torn opening was too small—ketchup would spurt in unexpected directions. In this way I managed to get ketchup on my shirt, the tabletop, and Jason's arm.

"Watch it," he complained.

"Sorry," I said. I gripped the portion of my shirt that had ketchup on it, held it up, and licked it.

"Gross," Jason said at the same moment that Shaun's mom, horrified, said, "Shaun!"

All right. No licking.

I grabbed a napkin and scrubbed at the ketchup instead. What a waste.

Shaun's mom had a salad in a plastic tray. It looked crisp and appealing, all different shades of green, with a few curls of purple and orange. And a few small, red round things scattered here and there.

She pulled out a larger version of a ketchup packet—this one had a man's face on it—and tore easily across the tiny line. "Jason," she said in a bright voice as she gently squeezed a white viscous substance from the packet onto her vegetables, "why don't you call Cameron after dinner and see if he wants to come over?"

Shaun's mom had been fussing over Jason and his lack of friends for years. She used to take charge by having boys from his class over to play. They seldom reciprocated. None of the kids liked Jason enough to ask if he could visit *them*. A few parents insisted that their sons return the invitation, but these parents then complained of the way Jason wouldn't look them in the eye, the way he tended to break toys, or the way he ate Fruit Roll-Ups and then absentmindedly dropped the empty wrappers wherever he stood.

Now Jason was thirteen. He was too old for his mother to actively attempt to maneuver his social life. And she was champing at the bit to do so, you could tell by the way her voice took on an encouraging tone. "What do you think?" she urged Jason.

I swirled a fry in ketchup, getting it nicely covered. The Cameron she spoke of was a boy Jason's age who lived three houses down. I thought it would be a terrible mistake to call him. Cameron was a sower of pain. He ate kids like Jason for breakfast.

Jason apparently agreed. "I don't want to."

"Why not?" Shaun's mom dropped the packet into one of the empty bags. "He seems nice enough."

"He threw erasers at me."

I watched Shaun's mom stir the salad with her small plastic fork, flipping the lettuce around expertly. I'd squirted my ketchup into a puddle next to my fries, like Jason had, but now I wished I'd put it directly on them and mixed it up with a fork. That made sense.

But there were no more plastic forks, alas. Only those with salad got forks.

I continued dipping and eating.

"That was in third grade, Jason," I heard Shaun's mom say. "You should give him another chance."

Jason and I both knew that he should *not* give Cameron another chance. Cameron would refuse to come over, then mock him at school the next day for daring to ask.

Of course, I couldn't say any of this. And all Jason said was "I don't want to" again.

Shaun's mom nodded, apparently engrossed in her mixing, but now her fork sent the lettuce leaping around her tray at an alarming rate.

"What about Benny?" she tried.

Benny lived a few blocks away. He cursed his parents to their faces, made hit lists, and looked up bombmaking on the Internet.

Shaun's mom would have had no way of knowing any of this. She would only see that Benny's mother was president of the PTA and made him tuck his shirts in.

"I don't want to," Jason said again. His standard non-communicative line.

Shaun's mom sighed. She looked worried, I thought. I felt bad for her. She was so concerned about her son—and clueless as to how to help him.

Thinking about it, I believed I knew a good possibility for a Jason friendship. There was an eighth-grade boy who lived not far from Bailey, who was shy, video-game friendly, and very uncoordinated. Just like Jason. They might enjoy each other's company.

I'd never really appreciated the problem, though, of how one might get two human beings to become friends with each other. Especially when both tended to avoid speech and eye contact.

"Jason," his mom said, "I know it's hard, but I wish you'd get out and socialize once in a while."

"I did," Jason said through his last mouthful of double cheeseburger.

"Don't talk with your mouth full. Did what?"

Jason chewed and swallowed. "Got out and socialized." He slid his chair back.

"When did you do that?"

Jason stood up. "After school."

"You need to ask if you can be excused."

"May I be excused?"

"Yes," she said. "What do you mean, got out"—too late, Jason was gone, and she was talking to the empty doorway—"and socialized?" Her voice died off. She sounded confused, as if this particular phrase must have a different meaning from the usual one, when Jason used it.

At this rate, she'd have to track him down, sit on him, and pull an explanation out of him word by word, on a string.

"He came with me to Bailey's house," I explained.

"Oh." She looked puzzled. "Why?"

"We invited him."

"You invited him to hang out with you and Bailey?"

"Yes."

She digested this information. "You know you're supposed to call and let me know where you are," she said, but I thought she sounded tentative, not angry. And then she said nothing for a while, but thoughtfully ate her salad.

"What are those?" I asked her, pointing.

She looked down. "Cherry tomatoes."

I looked at the remaining unsquished packets. "Tomato Ketchup," they said.

"May I try one?" I asked.

"A tomato? Sure."

I watched as she tried to stab it. It shot out from under her fork. Then she tried scooping, but it rolled away. Finally she grabbed the tomato with her fingers and handed it to me: "Here." She sounded irritated.

I popped it into my mouth and bit down. Juices exploded onto my tongue. Disappointing. It didn't taste the least bit ketchupy. Definitely not worth the chase it required.

Must be, I reflected, *it's the other ingredients that give ketchup its flavor. The spices and sugars and other things.*

Still, I chewed and swallowed the tomato. It did have interesting textures.

Shaun's mom appeared to be deep in thought. I decided not to bother her, and silently finished my fries and burger before slurping the last drops of Coke out of the bottom of my cup. Then I gathered up the trash and prepared to take it into the kitchen and dispose of it.

"May I be excused?" I asked politely.

Shaun's mom nodded. But when I stood up, she said quickly, "Shaun."

I paused.

"That was a very nice thing to do, taking your brother with you today. Did he enjoy it?"

"Seemed to."

"I *really* appreciate it. He has such a hard time making

friends," she added, and I could tell she was fretting about Jason, because she started stirring her salad again.

"Would you like me to invite him again tomorrow?" I offered magnanimously.

"Yes, if you can. It's not putting a cramp in your style, is it?"

"I don't have much of a style to cramp," I pointed out, and turned to go. If Peanut had moved on, I wanted to sit in Shaun's room and correct a test he'd failed. The answers had to be marked on a sheet that had hundreds of tiny circles on it. I would get to select circles and bubble them in. I was looking forward to it.

"You're a good kid, Shaun," I heard Shaun's mom say as I passed.

I hesitated. I had the feeling that this moment required something of me, some reciprocal words or gesture.

I put one hand on her shoulder and patted it awkwardly. It was the best I could do.

She looked a little surprised, but then she smiled and lifted one hand to place it briefly on mine. It felt bony, and the fingers were cold.

Bodies are rather untidy, with a somewhat gummy saclike skin holding organs in place so they won't fall out, the whole thing oozing sweat and oil and constantly shedding dead cells. Physical contact is just plain odd, when you get down to it.

That's why I was surprised to find that I liked it.

Bubbling in tests sounded like fun, and it was—for about ten minutes. I tried using different pencil strokes and techniques, but it seems there are only so many ways to fill a tiny circle with graphite leavings. Still, I finished the assignment and then did Shaun's geometry homework. That wasn't much more fun, but I felt I ought to complete Shaun's obligations.

By the time I was done, Jason and his mother had both gone to bed. I thought I should get into bed, too— but then I remembered how Bailey had chastised me that morning for not getting online.

It didn't sound very interesting, talking via a keyboard and a screen. I'd much rather talk to someone face-to-face and watch their flesh slide, shift, and twitch from muscular expansion and contraction.

However, this was Shaun's life. I was determined to at least *try* to follow its structure.

I turned on Shaun's computer. It hummed quietly, as if coming to life. I sighed and brought up Instant Messenger.

Bloo-bloo-bloop! said the computer, and a little box popped up.

fullmetal7bd: hey dude hows ur face?

That was Bailey.

I started to write "It's sore, but better than it was," but I'd had no practice in keyboarding. Shaun was a good typist, and I knew where the keys were, but again, knowing was not the same as doing. I had to keep looking down in order to put my fingers in the proper location. It was taking too long, so I finally just wrote:

trojanxxl: fine

fullmetal7bd: what r u doin*?*

I pecked out "Stuff," but as I clicked on SEND—*Bloo-bloo-bloop!*—another box popped up. I knew that Shaun often carried on several conversations at once, so I turned my attention to the new box:

angeloftheLord: Kiriel, you are trespassing in direct contravention of the Creator's wishes. This is a warning: Return to your duties or you will be punished.

14

All the warmth had left my fingertips.

> **trojanxxl:** who is this?

Bloo-bloo-bloop!

> **angeloftheLord:** You must return to your duties
> immediately.

An eternity of wishing to speak directly to my Creator, I
thought in despair—*and this is how He finally contacts me?
Through AOL Instant Messenger?*

But no. "Angel of the Lord": that would not be the
Creator Himself. It would be one of His lieutenants.

Gabriel, Michael, Raphael—someone like that.

That's how you know you're low on the list. When you don't even rate a face-to-face meeting with an underling.

trojanxxl: With whom am I speaking?

Is that right? I thought. *"Whom" is a direct object: "I am speaking to whom."*

Yes, that's right.

I hit SEND.

"angeloftheLord is offline," said the little box.

fullmetal7bd: r u still there?

trojanxxl: got to go. bye.

I logged off and shut the computer down. I wasn't about to touch it again. And I wouldn't go to sleep tonight, not until this body zonked out on its own.

They'll have to drag me out of here, I thought.

Then I realized: *They're going to.*

Strange how one can feel satisfaction, dread, and fear at the same time.

Now I felt as if I were being watched. I reached to turn

off the desk lamp, immersing the room in darkness. It made me feel better, as if anybody trying to find me now would be as blind as I was.

My human eyes adjusted to the lack of light, and shapes began to form as the dark became shades of black and gray. The house was quiet. The bedroom window appeared to be glowing behind the blinds, a lovely muted silvery cast.

I stepped over Shaun's scattered CDs to his window and pulled the cord to raise the blinds. As I did so, a flurry of dust rose into my face.

Immediately I had a tickling in my nose, an odd sensation that the nose was drawing me into action whether I willed it or not. A feeling of inevitability . . .

"Ahhh-*choo!*"

A sneeze. I'd sneezed! It was as compelling and as irresistible as ejaculation—of course, not nearly as much fun, but it was *physical*. It was something I'd gotten to experience before the Creator sent His Unfallen henchmen for me.

I was happy to feel the tickling again, the dawning need. Another sneeze was coming down the pipeline.

This time I wanted to see if it really was unavoidable. I opened my eyes wide and wrinkled up my nose, fighting it. . . .

"Ahh-*choo!*"

Marvelous!

I waited, but nothing else happened, and as nothing had come out of my nose that required attention, I went ahead and opened Shaun's window. A screen stood between me and the outside, but I could smell and feel the night air.

I dragged Shaun's amplifier over and sat on it, propping my elbows on the windowsill. I immediately saw that the silvery glow came from the moon. It was all reflected light, the hot golden light of day turned cool and ethereal in its windings through space.

Funny how there could be such a difference between air and . . . *air*. Inside, I could smell specific odors, like Shaun's sweat stains, or Peanut's litterbox, or the greasy smell of the French fries we'd had for dinner. But this night air from outside had a thousand subtle smells to it, most of which I didn't have enough experience to identify. I thought one was the scent of fresh grass. Another might be damp soil.

The rest? I'd probably never know. I'd have to go back before I found out.

Shaun's lungs heaved in and out with *my* breath. A slight breeze from outside teased the tiny hairs on Shaun's arms—but *I* was the one who felt them. *I* felt. *I* saw. *I* heard. *I* tasted.

I got to experience something besides secondhand misery.

And I loved it.

I sighed, and rested my chin on my elbows. This body was already getting that heavy-eyed, foggy-brained feeling that meant it needed sleep.

Sleep. What a waste. And this time, it was likely that I wouldn't awaken in this world.

The moon, with its pale gray, seemed to blur and dim.

I thought: *Am I crying?*

I darted my eyes from side to side, trying to see tears. The blurriness was definitely there, but when I lifted my fingers to my cheeks, they were dry.

I squeezed my eyes shut and felt the rims and lashes; sure enough, there were a few drops of moisture! *I did cry a little*, I thought with satisfaction.

I tried to cry some more, but to no avail. Finally, I stood and shut the window. And as I pulled the shade down, I admitted what I already knew: No matter what happened, this holiday was worth it. It was worth any-thing to be able to cry real tears, to smell Lane's scent, to feel a cherry tomato burst on my tongue—even having my fingertips slashed added spice and depth, because it led me to feel things, and to think things, that I might not have, otherwise.

And if, after I was done, it turned out that I had attracted the notice of the Creator, that would indeed be a fitting end to a lovely vacation.

I headed down the darkened hall to the bathroom, feeling an odd mixture of joy and sadness. There were so many things I still longed to do. Small things, like hot baths and soft carpets and sex.

I just wanted to stay, that's all—just a bit longer. I'd barely been here one day. It wasn't enough.

Not nearly enough.

*. . . and the evening and the
morning were the second day . . .*

15

The first thing I became aware of was infinite darkness.

Second thing: I could not move. I was captured, trussed. My arms and legs bound.

My *arms*?

My *legs*?

I opened my eyes, and the darkness became forest green paint.

I was still here. I was in Shaun's bed, lying on my side, staring at the wall.

I looked down. The sheets had become tangled around my limbs in the night.

I got to see another morning!

"Woo-hoo!" I shouted to Peanut, who sat on the dresser, watching me. This time I didn't care who heard me.

Peanut just stared, expressionless.

"The repo men haven't come yet," I told him. "Get it? *Repo*-ssession? Although technically this wasn't a possession in the first place. But you know that, right? You're a very sharp cat."

Peanut remained unimpressed.

He didn't move, but watched as I got dressed.

My removal was imminent. But now that it was morning, an irresistible idea began to bubble up.

It looked to me like I might have a chance to quickly slip in one or two tiny nudges to this plane before I left.

I bet I could manage it, too—just leave a couple of small marks, nothing that would hurt anyone, nothing that would interrupt the space-time continuum. Just a few teensy asterisks that would linger after I was gone, the way a boy deep in the woods carves an initial in a tree trunk that no one will ever see: KIRIEL WAS HERE.

I'd have to think what I wanted to do exactly, but I knew I wanted to try *something*.

I kept my distance from Peanut so as not to annoy him, but when I was fully clothed I moved a *little* closer to him—not much—and studied him curiously. His paws were white, as was the front of his chest and his throat. The rest of his fur had appeared to have smooth, perfect brown stripes, but now I could see that the stripes blurred and overlapped at the edges, looking both soft and jagged at the same time. I longed to put out a finger and touch them.

But I didn't.

When I went into the kitchen, Shaun's mom was digging in her purse. A small mound of Kleenex and papers and makeup supplies lay heaped on the counter next to it. "Morning," she said, adding a wallet to the pile. "You're up a little early."

"Indeed I am."

She found what she was looking for—her keys—and pulled them out of the purse. "Did you have a bad dream this morning?" she asked, stuffing everything else back in. "I thought I heard you calling out."

"No, no bad dreams. I slept well."

"That's good. Listen," she said in a lowered voice, with a glance over my shoulder, "don't forget about inviting Jason to Bailey's."

Oh. Right. "I won't forget," I told her.

"And would you remind him to take his meds when he comes in?"

"Okay."

She beamed, and headed for the back door. "Wonderful. Have a good day, all right?"

"You, too," I said, but she was already gone.

I proceeded to get two bowls and two spoons out. I poured myself some Froot Loops, and Jason some

Cinnamon Toast Crunch. The individual pieces of cereal seemed to blur as they slid into the bowl.

As I was pouring the milk, Jason appeared, fully dressed, although with untied shoelaces and mussed hair.

"Here." I handed him his cereal. He grunted something unintelligible, but took it and carried it over to the table, where he grabbed the spoon and dug in, eating silently.

I took the seat next to him. I'd quite been looking forward to more Froot Loops, and today I tasted them one by one, testing to see if each color had a different flavor. It did, so I sorted and pushed the pieces with my spoon until I was able to shovel a whole pile of yellows into my mouth at once.

This took a bit of time, and Jason was finishing up before I remembered to ask him, "Hey, you want to come to Bailey's with me after school today?"

Jason shrugged.

"Is that a yes or no?"

He shrugged again. "I know I'm not as good as you guys," he said, not looking at me.

I thought about it for a moment. He must be referring to the video game the three of us had played together.

"You're better than I am," I told him truthfully.

"No, I'm not."

"You were yesterday." I didn't add that he always

would be, from now on. "And you beat Bailey once, too."

Jason gave no indication that he'd heard. He pushed his chair back with a screech and got up. He took his empty cereal bowl to the sink and dropped it. There was a brief clatter as it hit the stainless steel, punctuated by another, rather alarming sound that might have been chipping glass. He hesitated, and I saw him dart me a furtive glance.

"Don't forget your medicine," I told him.

Jason moved quickly away from the sink, as if he had nothing to do with anything that lay there, and grabbed a small brown plastic bottle from its place on the counter. It was always on the counter, because Shaun's mom said that Jason had a better chance of remembering it if it was in plain view. He was quite the expert at taking pills—he had one out of the bottle and down his throat, no water, in less than two seconds.

"So," I said as he recapped the bottle and set it down, "I'll see you after school."

"Okay," he said with a shrug.

He certainly didn't utilize much facial or vocal expression in communicating with other people. He didn't even use many words. I could see now, after having been here a while, how people would think he didn't care about things.

I thought he *did* care, though. His methods of communication were smaller than other humans', but that didn't mean they weren't there. I thought, *If he speaks to me again—if he actually says good-bye to his brother before he leaves the house—that means he's experiencing some camaraderie.*

So as he moved across the kitchen, I said nothing, just sorted and ate my Froot Loops. But I was listening.

"See you," Jason muttered as he walked out the door without looking around.

I didn't bother speaking; he was already gone. But I detected some facial movement and put my fingers up to my face.

No teeth were uncovered. But the corners of my mouth had risen slightly. Not a grin. Just a small smile.

"You're kinda quiet, dude," Bailey said on the bus.

"Uh-huh," I said. I *was* quiet. I had a lot to think about, and quickly. There were things to be attempted—*K*'s to be carved—before I was dragged out of this existence. "I guess I'm tired," I lied, hoping that Bailey would let it go.

He did. He pulled out a handful of index cards with writing on them and began flipping through, staring at each. I recognized them as English vocabulary.

I settled into the seat, thinking. There was only a short time left, and I was unwilling to play havoc with Shaun's friends and family. I wanted to leave only subtle, but satisfying, traces behind.

There were three main tree trunks I thought I could put a *K* on.

So. First "tree." "There's something I want to ask you," I told Bailey.

"Go ahead," he said absently, frowning over his cards.

"If anything ever happens to me, would you watch out for Jason?"

Bailey looked up. *"What?"*

"If I—um, got hurt. Or, you know, if I . . . if I *died*, would you do me a favor and just kind of keep an eye on Jason? Help him out, check up on him?"

Bailey was looking at me so steadily now that he reminded me of Peanut. "Is there something going on I need to know about?"

I thought he sounded suspicious, so I deliberately turned to face him and made full eye contact.

"No," I said.

"You're not, like, sick or anything?"

"No."

"You sure?"

"Yeah. It's just a favor, that's all."

"That's a really weird thing to be asking."

"Okay, but will you?"

"Yeah, sure." He turned back to his vocabulary cards. "Whatever."

Death was not something Shaun or Bailey had discussed before. My guess was that Bailey had seldom even thought about it. Now he seemed thoughtful and a little sober as he stared down at the cards in his lap.

So. I'd begun with Jason; there was nothing more I could do at the moment. Now I would immerse myself in the matter of Lane.

"Shaun?" I heard Bailey ask in a somber voice.

"Yeah?"

"If anything ever happens to me, would you do me a favor?"

"Sure."

"Would you make sure they bury me with my bobble-head collection?"

"I'll make sure," I solemnly promised. Feeling terrible, because of course I wouldn't be around when Bailey died.

Then I saw that Bailey was smirking at me.

Had he been *joking*?

I tried to picture it: Bailey lying in a long box with his arms crossed, surrounded by dozens of bouncing large-headed figurines.

It *was* a joke.

"Very funny," I said.

"Man, you thought I was serious." Bailey snickered,

bending over his cards again. "What an ass. It's quite salient to me," he added, eyeing his cards, "that you're a reprehensible and credulous ass."

He'd misused "salient." I shook my head and turned to stare out the window.

"Tree" number two: Lane.

I was quite looking forward to achieving sexual gratification with her—but after giving it some thought, I also felt that I could tweak the situation to do double duty.

Yes, I would use her as an instrument to fulfill my desires. But I would be *her* desire-fulfilling instrument as well.

I would make Shaun Simmons one of the best experiences of her life.

Lane didn't know how lucky she was. Unlike many teenage boys, I had the knowledge necessary to create a sublime first sexual experience for a girl. It wouldn't be any trouble; indeed, it would likely increase my enjoyment as well.

So. It had to be after school. There would be no opportunities at school to consummate our love. I would get her alone. Then I'd do everything just the way she'd written it in her diary. We'd follow one of her already imagined scenarios and fall into each other's arms. Then we'd have intercourse, and when we were finished, she'd be left with a lingering memory that she'd recall with joy for the rest of her days.

Let's see, what *had* she written in her journal? It was hard to remember; there had been several versions. There was one where Shaun asked her to a school dance—that was out of the question, of course, because there was no school dance to go to. There was one where Shaun said nothing, but smiled at her with "sparkling eyes." I didn't know how to do that. It sounded exciting, though. I made a mental note to keep watch for sparkling eyes today, in case I could see how it was done.

There was the version where Shaun told her she was beautiful.

Oh. That was the one.

Bailey's lips moved silently as he read over his cards. I realized that the bus had come quite a way, but I hadn't noticed the landscape going by. I had been looking out the window the whole time, but hadn't *seen* anything. It was as if concentrating heavily on something else had made my brain skip over all visual input.

Now I focused, and the first thing I saw was a church. I knew it was a church because there was a sign out front: FIRST METHODIST.

I hadn't seen it yesterday. I must have been looking out the other side of the bus when we passed. The building was rather blockish, and seemed to be made of a featureless white cement.

Was it truly a holy place? Was the Creator there more than He was in other places? Did He use it to achieve a connection with humans that was denied to other beings?

I turned and watched it disappear into the distance.

I spent English figuring out the logistics of my afternoon with Lane. I'd go to her again as she passed from her geometry class to her science class. I'd smile as much as possible, since she seemed to like that. I'd ask her to come to my—to Shaun's—house after school. I'd make sure Jason was busy with his video games. I'd take Lane into the bedroom, tell her she was beautiful, get both of us stripped down, then launch into a union of heart and body that would be awe inspiring in its scope and intensity. Simple enough.

Yes, I was quite looking forward to it.

The bell rang, and I gathered up Shaun's things. As I was passing the teacher's desk, he called to me.

"Shaun. Can you stay a moment?"

I said nothing, still being deep in thought, but I obediently went to him.

"I started grading yesterday's quizzes," he said, "and I want to talk to you about yours."

"All right."

He reached down and picked up a stack of papers. "You made a *one hundred* on this quiz," he said, looking at the paper on top.

"Yes, I see that."

"I have to admit that I find it a little odd, since you've barely managed to pull low C's all year." He tossed the papers back onto the desk and folded his arms. "I'm going to be moving your seat, Shaun. Away from Mindy Parsons."

"All right."

He stared at me. "Shaun. Be honest. Did you read the play?"

I started to say that technically speaking, no, I did not read it. But I saw that Mr. Collins suspected Shaun of cheating and that this entire interview was pointless, since Shaun was not here and I already knew the contents of the play.

"Yes, I did," I told him. Shaun actually died without having read the play, but no matter. I wanted to leave this room and go about my business.

"Then you wouldn't mind if I asked you a few questions about it right now."

"I need to get to my next class."

"Just a couple of very quick questions."

"All right, then. Go ahead."

He leaned back against his desk and folded his arms. "Tell me about it."

"What do you want to know?"

He shrugged. "How about you tell me the title first."

The Crucible.

"What's it about?"

"On the surface, it's about the Salem Witch Trials, in which a group of lying teenage girls claimed to be possessed by Satan's minions." I still found the whole thing laughably insulting. "However, it can also be read as a metaphor for the McCarthy hearings of the 1950s."

"What about the main character. Who is it?"

"I would say John Proctor."

"Okay. So. Tell me what happens to John Proctor."

"Among other things, his wife is accused of witchcraft. There is some difficulty because he has had an affair with one of the accusing girls. His wife could clear herself by admitting in public that he has done this thing, but she won't, and so she is lost. John Proctor himself is then accused and, in the end, hangs for a crime of which he is innocent." I looked steadily at Mr. Collins, waiting for the next question.

But he didn't ask. His gaze, which had been intent and accusing, wavered.

"All right," Mr. Collins said after a moment. "I'll let this grade stand. But if I so much as glimpse your eyes moving an *inch* in the direction of somebody else's paper, I'm going to flunk you, pronto. *Capisce?*"

"Yes, that seems fair. But you know," I remarked, because I felt it should be pointed out, "sometimes students *do* make a commitment to work harder."

"Not often."

"But sometimes."

"Very rarely."

"But *sometimes*."

"Well . . . maybe." He glanced at the stack of papers on his desk and seemed to droop a little. "Yes, maybe *sometimes* they do."

I waited a moment, but he didn't say anything. "Are we done?" I asked.

"Yes. You can go now."

"All right," I said, pulling Shaun's backpack over my shoulder. "Thank you for your time." I added, heading for the door.

"Shaun?"

I turned around.

"Don't be a smart aleck."

I was about to say, *Yes sir*, but then, thinking better of it, I just nodded. I wanted to get to Lane before she was gone.

"Hi," I said as I caught up with her in the hall.

She turned around, her lovely hair sliding over her shoulders. I didn't know as much about human expressions as I should have, but I was getting better at it, and it was clear that her face changed when she saw that it was me. Or rather, when she thought she saw Shaun. At any rate, I saw why it was said that people's faces "glowed" when they were happy. Lane was *glowing* now.

The sparkling-eye thing, not so much.

"Hi." Her voice sounded breathless.

"I was wondering," I said very calmly—even though I could actually feel the heart pounding against my lungs and ribs as I spoke—"if you'd like to come over to my house after school today."

"What for?"

"For . . ." I hesitated, thinking.

Don't say "mutual sexual fulfillment." It'll ruin everything.

". . . homework," I finished. "I was hoping you could help me with my homework."

"In what?"

"English." Then I remembered that Lane hadn't been doing so well in English, last I'd seen. "Geometry," I added.

"Um. Which is it?"

"Geometry," I said firmly. "I'm having trouble with geometry."

"Sure, I'll come. Your mom or dad'll be there, right?"

"Shau— my dad doesn't live with us. My mom doesn't get off work till six."

"I can't come over till after six, then. My mom won't let me go to somebody's house unless an adult is there."

Shaun's backpack was digging into my shoulders. I gave it a heave, trying to shift it a little.

I'd forgotten about Lane's mother's rules. They *did* complicate things.

"You don't have to tell your mom," I pointed out, knowing that this approach was probably futile.

Indeed it was. Lane pulled her books against her chest. "I can't *lie*," she said, looking a little bewildered at the thought.

Lane, Lane, you honest girl. How I adore you!

"You could come to *my* house," she said.

No, I could not. Lane's grandmother lived there, and not only would she *not* leave us alone, she wouldn't even let me in Lane's *room*. She would make us sit at the dining room table with her while she drank a glass of buttermilk and told stories about her childhood.

I thought quickly. I had to do this ASAP. I didn't know when the hammer would fall, so to speak.

"How about if we meet at Bailey's house," I suggested. "His mother is home after school."

"You and I would do homework at Bailey's?"

"Yes. Your mother knows Bailey's mother, does she not? And trusts her?"

"Does she not," Lane repeated, her mouth twisting into a smile.

"What's funny?"

"Nothing. I guess maybe Bailey's house would be all right," she added. "Bailey's okay with that?"

"Yes," I said, joy swelling inside my chest. Bailey was a friend who approved of my quest. He'd make sure Lane and I had time alone.

"You invited Lane Henneberger to *my* house," Bailey echoed. "Without asking *me*?"

We were standing in the lunch line, waiting to be served something on a round bun. I perceived ketchup packets on the trays of people farther down the line, and felt a flutter of anticipation.

"Why'd you do that?" Bailey complained.

"I have no chance at a union with Lane in her house," I pointed out.

"You have no chance at a union with Lane in *my* house, dude. And unless I've missed something, you barely even *know* Lane."

"I know her very well."

"Yeah? When's the last time you talked to her?"

"This afternoon."

"Before . . . this week. When's the last time you said anything to Lane Henneberger before this week?"

"I don't remember."

"The last time I know of was back in second grade. Remember we yelled 'Banzai!' and threw water balloons at her in the street?"

"Are you refusing to let her come over?"

"I don't *care* if she comes over. You're totally missing the point."

Bailey was the one missing the point. And I couldn't explain it to him. He hadn't seen Lane pining for Shaun, hadn't seen her writing lustful pages about the way Shaun's hair curled on the back of his neck. She loved Shaun, and was more than ready to demonstrate her feelings. As I was ready to demonstrate mine.

I sighed. "Okay, Bailey, what's the point I'm missing?"

"Even if she *would* let you get in her pants, you aren't going to have a chance to try."

"All you have to do is leave us alone in your room for a little while."

"What do you think, my mom and I are going to wait in the driveway while you seduce her?"

"Oh, yeah." I remembered. "Your mom."

"Duh!" Bailey's mother never minded teenagers coming into her house. She never minded if they ate her food and stayed for hours. She just always seemed to have one eye and ear on them.

"Hmm. That *could* be a problem. I've already invited Lane, though." I thought about it. "If the three of us are in your room, could you go for a snack and not come back for, say, an hour?"

"No."

"Thirty minutes?"

"And what do you want me to tell my mother when she asks why I'm hanging around the kitchen while you two are in my room with the door shut?"

"That you're very hungry?"

"Shaun. Think with your head and not your nuts. *It's not going to work.*"

Logically speaking, I knew he was right. Still, I felt positive about the outcome. Somehow I would manage to get time alone with my Lane.

"Well," I said, unable to come up with any other ideas on the spur of the moment, "why don't we proceed as planned, then, and just keep an eye out for the opportunity which may present itself?"

"*We?*"

"Okay, *I* will proceed as planned. Lane and I will come over to your house to do homework."

"I totally don't care. Just don't expect anything from me. *Or* my mom."

"I won't."

"And do you know how weird you've been talking?"

"No," I began, but then I realized what he meant was that I had not been using Shaun's grammatical patterns.

I was starting to slip.

"Whatever," I said quickly.

But Bailey was already shaking his head as he picked up his tray.

16

When I sat down at our table, my tray held a hamburger and a small mound of French fries, but only four ketchup packets. The stingy net-head behind the counter wouldn't give me more than that.

"Can I have your ketchup?" I asked Bailey.

"No."

I sighed. I rather enjoyed sighing.

I carefully tore one packet and squished the ketchup out, onto my fries. I had a fork today, and would try Shaun's mom's salad-stirring method.

As I reached for a second packet, I glanced up and saw the sower of pain loading up his tray in the lunch line.

Reed McGowan. The third "tree."

It nagged at me, having such close access to him.

Being in his physical presence right *now*, having a chance to communicate with him while he was actively committing his sins. *Not* interminably reliving those sins via his pathetic, whining soul when the sins were old, stale, and carved in stone.

I couldn't give up on him yet. A small flame of hope burned in me, an almost human kind of hope. Here I was, outside of the usual rules that bound me. And I wanted to *keep trying*.

Bailey turned to see what had captured my attention. He turned back quickly.

"Tell me," he said, "that you're not looking at Reed McGowan."

"But I *am* looking at Reed McGowan."

Bailey gave a quick glance over his shoulder again. "He's not doing anything to anybody."

"He did, though. And he will."

"But he's not *now*. So quit looking at him."

But I couldn't. There stood a walking pile of cruelty, guilt, insecurity, and childishness.

Reed McGowan: my future.

"Come on," Bailey said, more urgently now. "Don't give him anything to start with."

He sounded so concerned that I hesitated a few moments, considering. But I wanted very much to get Reed moving away from the bowels of Hell—or at least *my* part of the bowels of Hell. If he ended up in somebody else's part, that was their lookout.

"I have to try," I told Bailey. "I have to talk to him."

"You're not serious. He'll kill you."

"Unlikely," I said. "He may hit me again, but I doubt he'll beat me to death." I wasn't going to be using this body much longer anyway. A few loose teeth would be worth cutting eons off Reed's company in the afterlife.

I pushed my chair back and got up.

"Aw, no," Bailey pleaded. "*No*, Shaun."

"It must be done," I said simply, and went to see Reed.

They say you can catch more flies with honey than with vinegar, I reflected as I headed across the cafeteria. Although what one would want to do with flies once caught, I do not know. Murder them, most likely—that seemed to me to be what humans generally did with caught flies. I suspected there was a lesson and a warning there about humans in general.

I didn't want to murder Reed. I wanted to change him, but I knew that wasn't possible.

All humans have free will. Reed was the only one who could do the changing.

In this case, all I could think to do was to plant a seed and hope it'd start growing on its own. A disappointingly small *K*, but surely better than nothing.

Reed was paying for his lunch. I observed that he had

not ketchup packets, but mayonnaise. Not milk, but iced tea. Otherwise, he had the same as everyone else: one hamburger, French fries, and a mixture of peas and carrots.

"Reed," I said, approaching him as the net-head handed him his change. "May I speak to you?"

He looked up, and when he saw who it was, his eyes narrowed.

"I want to apologize," I told him, "for what I said yesterday. I wasn't thinking how it might make you feel."

Reed kept his eyes on me, but didn't say anything. I had no idea what he might be thinking.

He looked away, and deliberately dropped his change into his pocket.

"Move on, please," said the net-head.

Reed scooped up his tray and started across the cafeteria.

I quickly caught up with him. "It concerns me," I said, walking beside him, "to see you treating other people the way you sometimes do. I'm guessing that at this point you don't particularly care how they feel about it."

That was silly. Of course he didn't care about making people feel bad. The sowers of pain never do—not till later. Sometimes much, much later.

I started over. "Do you care how it reflects on *you* when you mistreat others?"

He still wouldn't look at me. In fact, he seemed to be pretending I wasn't even there. The only thing he said was a snarled "Outta my way" to a knot of girls who were standing in the aisle.

"When people hear you speak like that," I pointed out, "they don't respect you. They certainly don't like you. If they even fear you, it's only the sort of fear they might feel for a mad dog."

The girls found their seats, and Reed continued on again. He was walking *very* quickly now. I had to trot to stay with him. I continued to speak in a low voice: "You may think, because you have friends, that you are liked. But teenagers are notoriously insecure, and for the most part your 'friends' must know that you could turn on them on a dime. On a *dime*," I said again, liking the sound of it. "Yes, you could turn on them on a dime."

We were almost to Reed's usual table, where his friends already sat. And finally Reed spoke.

"Get away from me," he said out of the side of his mouth.

"All right," I agreed, out of the side of my mouth as well. "I just wanted to give you something to think about. If you want to have *real* friends, you might want to consider whether your actions are those of someone who can be trusted and relied upon."

Reed finally stopped. I did, too. I felt oddly light and

pleased, as if the act of speaking my mind had somehow removed a weight I'd been carrying.

He stood there, still holding his tray, staring down at me with his upper lip slightly curled. I couldn't tell if he had been touched by my words or if he wanted to hit me again.

I found myself hunching into my shoulders a little, in case our encounter took the hitting direction.

"You," Reed McGowan told me with complete conviction, "are a total *freak*." Then he stepped over to his friends, put his tray on the table, and sat down. Our interview was over.

I didn't realize I'd been holding my breath until I let it out.

I'd said exactly what needed to be said—and he hadn't hit me! That could be because we were still in an area supervised by adults.

But it could mean that he had been *listening*.

In either case, I had sown my seed. That seed now had a chance to take root.

I unhunched my shoulders and walked back to Bailey.

Perhaps later, during a quiet time, Reed would reflect on what I said. If he did reflect, there was only one conclusion he could come to.

Another *K* begun.

17

It was on the way home that I remembered Jason was supposed to accompany me to Bailey's this afternoon.

Well, I'd just tell him to stay home. My chances of having time alone with Lane were already shaky. They would shrink to solid nothing if Jason was with me.

It wasn't as if I were going to be around to make a habit of being there for him, anyway. The kid would be back in his solitary routine before you could say "Shaun is dead."

When I walked into Shaun's living room, Jason was in his usual spot in front of the television, controller in hand. He didn't look up when I entered. I would have thought he hadn't noticed, except that he spoke.

"You're late," he said without turning around.

I turned to look at the clock over the mantel. Shaun

usually got home around three thirty; it was now three thirty-five.

"I thought maybe you went straight over to Bailey's." That was a long sentence, for Jason.

Had he been looking forward to this afternoon?

I knew I must *immediately* tell him that he was dis-invited.

"Um," I said instead. "How was school?"

Jason said nothing. His fingers—well, his thumb, mostly—kept moving on the controller, and I stood there with Shaun's backpack over one shoulder, watching him destroy three aliens in a shower of purple goo. When the aliens were gone, I waited for him to guide his soldier around the corner where, I felt sure, there would be more aliens, some of them the type with claws who shot blue laserlike blasts that shattered their victims into a million pieces.

Instead, the scene froze. A square appeared on the screen, and inside it were words: "Continue." "Options." "Go to Menu." "Quit Game." These words denoted choices for Jason to make.

He didn't make them. Instead, he actually turned around and looked directly at me.

"Why are you being so nice to me all of a sudden?" he asked.

Me? *Nice?*

"I don't think I've been particularly nice," I told him. "I've been . . . civil."

Jason just eyed me. "Uh-huh," he said, but his voice and posture and facial expression radiated . . . what was it?

Suspicion.

"We hate each other," Jason told me. "Remember? You're not supposed to be civil."

"I don't hate you."

Jason stared at me for a moment. Then he made a strange sound—something like *shee-ah,* only through his nose more than his mouth so that it was half snort, half word—and went back to blowing away aliens.

I needed to leave the backpack in Shaun's room, then head out to meet Lane at Bailey's. Instead, I stood there watching Jason's back, thinking. I didn't believe that Shaun had really hated Jason. It was more likely just irritation that had become cruel habit.

On the other hand, it seemed to me that Jason had come pretty close to hating Shaun. It hadn't started that way, as I recalled; it seemed like it had started with Jason bugging Shaun.

Why had he bugged Shaun?

Boredom?

Admiration?

Wanting attention?

All three?

Looking at Jason's back—which, really, was what Shaun must have mostly seen of him—I felt suddenly tired. In my line of work, I'd known countless siblings who'd grown apart without ever having actually known each other. By the time they got to me, it was far too late for them to do anything about their regrets.

Well, I thought, *I'm* not *Jason's sibling. It's not my problem, and I can't solve it.*

Still . . .

"I don't hate you, Jason," I told him again.

He snorted again. "It's not like you invited me to go with you today because you *like* me."

He hadn't taken his eyes off the screen. He'd spoken with utter belief.

So how was it that the last words hung in the air and made it into a question?

They hung there, and then they fell into place all around me, an unintended trap. I *had* invited Jason because I liked him. If I now told him to stay home, my actions would confirm his statement.

I turned away and fled to Shaun's room, where I tossed Shaun's backpack aside before shutting the door and leaning back against it.

A strange emotion boiled within me, born of conflicting urges. Was it frustration? I couldn't quite figure it out.

I could do anything I wanted. I certainly had a choice whether to take Jason along. No one was forcing me.

Still, the feeling seethed. It seemed to require some kind of vent in order to be eased.

I'll curse, I decided. *Yes. I will let Jason come, but first I will curse. That will get the frustration out of my system.*

But none of the words I knew seemed like they would satisfy. Most American curse words seem to be related to perfectly natural bodily functions, and I've never seen why they strike people as being wicked. They didn't strike *me* as being particularly fufilling anyway. The only word commonly used that indeed felt like a curse was one that started with a *d* and ended with *mn*, and I had *no* desire to use that. No human would let it cross his lips if he knew what it meant in truly practical terms.

"Rats!" I tried. "Confound it! Egad! Tarnation! Blast!"

"Blast!" seemed to work pretty well, so I stuck with that. "Blast! Blast! Blast!" I pounded my fists against my thighs with each repetition. I didn't say it very loudly—didn't have to. It seemed that the pleasure of cursing wasn't about volume, but about vehemence.

After a while, I thought I did feel a *little* better. At the very least, it had distracted me.

I straightened, ran a hand through my hair à la Jason, took a deep breath and let it out. I noticed that even now, I still had a twinge of hope that my plans might work out.

Not likely—but it *was* still slightly possible.

Was this the hope that they say springs eternal in the human breast?

I went back into the living room.

"So," I said pleasantly to Jason, "you coming or what?"

18

"Good afternoon, Mrs. Darnell," I said when Bailey's mom answered the door. My only infinitesimal last pathetic chance at achieving union with my darling today was in the hands of a slightly overweight, slightly untidy housewife who had already raised three sons besides Bailey and who, unfortunately, was not stupid.

"Hi, Jason," she said, holding the door open. "And *good afternoon*, Shaun," she told me as we came in. "So. Why do you sound like Eddie Haskell, and why do you look like butter wouldn't melt in your mouth?"

"It's a good day to be alive," I told her.

"Yes, it is," Mrs. Darnell agreed, without missing a beat.

Bailey came ambling across the living room. "Hey," he

greeted me and Jason. "Oh, Mom. Shaun might need to study a little bit. Is it okay if he goes in Dad's office for some privacy?"

Bailey, may the Creator bless him, was making a last-ditch effort to provide me with a love nest.

"*Shaun* wants to study?" Mrs. Darnell repeated, her voice rising at the end. She looked me up and down. "Shouldn't he have brought some books, then?"

Oops.

"And what's wrong with *your* room, anyway?" Mrs. Darnell asked Bailey.

"Jason and I are going to be playing Tec Warriors in there."

"Then Shaun can use the kitchen counter. You know your dad doesn't like kids in his study."

The kitchen counter did not sound to me like a promising place to achieve spiritual and physical union. The kitchen opened onto three other rooms.

Behind me, the doorbell rang. "You get it," Bailey told me, but his mother was already opening the door.

"Um, hi." It was Lane's melodious, lilting voice. "I'm here to study? With Shaun?"

"Oh. Sure. Come on in," Mrs. Darnell said, evidently unperturbed.

I beamed at Lane as she entered, a book and a folder cradled against her chest.

Bailey's mom eyed Bailey. Then she turned her head and eyed *me* for a moment. I knew she had to be much better at reading me than I was at reading her. "Uh-huh," she said, apparently about nothing, and in a tone I couldn't identify. Then she added, "Lane, you and Shaun are going to come work in the kitchen." Her voice was pleasant but firm. "You'll have room to spread out in there."

I looked at Bailey. *A valiant effort, my friend. But it's time to throw in the towel.* "All right," I told his mother, officially giving up.

It was disappointing, but not unbearably so. Being in Lane's presence set all my senses humming.

Mrs. Darnell led the way into the kitchen. Lane followed her. I followed Lane. It was odd how being so close to her made me feel as if I were floating.

Lane and I climbed onto barstools while Mrs. Darnell opened a cabinet and started fishing around in it. "I know Shaun likes Cheetos. We also have pretzels, carrot sticks, and Ding Dongs. What would you like, Lane?"

"Nothing for me, thanks." Lane set her book and folder on the counter. "Didn't you bring your geometry stuff?" she asked me.

"I forgot." I saw Mrs. Darnell eyeing me again as she slid the Cheetos across the counter.

"Do you want to go get it?" Lane asked.

"Not really."

"Lane, Coke or Pepsi?" Mrs. Darnell asked.

"Thanks, but I'm not thirsty."

"Shaun?"

"Pepsi," I said. I'd already had Coke last night.

Mrs. Darnell handed me a blue can from the refrigerator, then headed out of the kitchen. I didn't open the can, and I didn't eat any Cheetos. Instead, I leaned on one elbow and watched Lane open her geometry folder. She pulled out a pencil that was tucked into the pocket.

"Anything in particular you want to start with?" she asked.

I could see Mrs. Darnell through the open doorway behind Lane, in the small laundry room next to the kitchen. She was pulling clothes out of a basket and putting them into a large white washing machine.

Lane sat so close that I could have easily leaned over and nibbled her ear. "Um," I said, wondering if it would alarm her if I touched her hair again. "You pick."

At that, I thought Lane looked slightly perplexed. Her brows furrowed a bit, at any rate. Her eyes were many shades of brown at once—a lighter color around the pupil, darkening around the rim of the iris.

She shrugged and started flipping through her book. "Well, what are you having trouble with?"

"Everything," I said, because "everything" would take more time. I leaned toward her, breathing in. Yes, there was that scent, faint and delicious.

"Maybe we should back up a bit, then." She frowned, still turning the pages. Her hands were exquisite, each finger ending in an oval nail, pink with a white crescent on the end. "Did you do okay with triangles?"

"Triangles," I agreed. Was this what it was like to be drunk? Her skin looked softer than anything I'd seen. I wanted to touch it with my fingertips, stroke her face and neck, run my hands over her bare abdomen and thighs. And I wanted to see her navel. The only one I'd seen so far was Shaun's.

"Did you understand the different kinds? Isosceles, equilateral, right?"

"Uh-huh."

"Okay. Well, what about the Pythagorean theorem?" She turned to look at me. "Did you have any trouble with that?"

I felt as if I were melting inside. "Explain it to me." It had become an effort for me to turn breath into words, because words suddenly seemed to be vague and foggy things.

Lane turned more pages until she found one she liked. "See the right angle?" she said, pointing. "The side across from that is the hypotenuse." As she talked, I watched the way her lips moved, forming sounds—hundreds of them, each one sliding effortlessly into another so that I couldn't have said where one ended and the next began. I waited for glimpses of her tongue and teeth, and thought how it might feel if they moved, licking and nipping, over my body.

Lane stopped. "Are you cold?"

"No."

"I thought you shivered."

"No," I lied.

"Do you remember the formula?"

"Which one?"

She put her hand over part of a page. "For the Pythagorean theorem."

"$a^2 + b^2 = c^2$."

"Okay, but what does that *mean*?"

"It means," I said, "that the sum of the squares of the sides of a right triangle is equal to the hypotenuse squared."

"Wow, you got that quick."

"You're a good teacher."

I thought she'd have liked to hear that, but she frowned down at the countertop. "Shaun," she said after a moment, "you don't really need help with geometry, do you?"

"No," I admitted.

"Then why did you ask me?"

"Because I wanted to be with you."

She fingered the edge of the book's page, her brow slightly furrowed again. "What do you mean, *be* with me?"

"To be in your presence."

Again, that thoughtful—no, *careful*—silence. Then: "Is this, like, supposed to be a joke?"

"No." It was odd that she wouldn't look at me. I didn't want her to be uncomfortable. I wanted to please her. "I think you're the most beautiful girl I've ever seen," I told her, taking the first step she'd outlined in her diary.

Now she looked up. But something wasn't right.

She appeared . . . *displeased*?

"Look," she said in a flat voice, "I *know* you're making fun of me."

"No," I said. "I'm not."

"I *know* I'm not beautiful."

"Of course you are."

"I am *not.*"

"You are." Why didn't she believe me? Because *she* didn't think she was beautiful? What did that have to do with *my* opinion? What did it have to do with reality?

"Mrs. Darnell," I said as Bailey's mom came back in, a round plastic basket of folded clothes balanced on one hip, "isn't Lane beautiful?"

Mrs. Darnell stopped. She looked Lane up and down. "Yes," she said firmly. "Very attractive. Especially the hair and eyes." She switched the basket to the other hip. "Are you two through? Because if you are, Shaun can help me out by taking this basket to Bailey."

"I'd better get going," Lane said, shutting her book and getting up.

"No!" I said. "Don't go. Please."

"We're done 'studying,' Shaun."

"But that doesn't mean you have to leave!" I felt as if all the air were being sucked out of the room.

Mrs. Darnell had been observing all this. Now she spoke up. "You don't have to rush off, Lane. Why don't the two of you go see what Bailey and Jason are up to?"

"That's right!" I said in desperation. "Hey. Come play Tectonic Warriors 2 with us!"

I saw one of Mrs. Darnell's eyebrows go up, but she didn't say anything.

"What's that?" Lane asked.

"It's a video game," Mrs. Darnell told her.

"I don't know how to play," Lane said. "I've hardly ever played *any* video games."

"Now's a good time to try it, then," Mrs. Darnell said lightly, handing me the laundry basket. "You have three experts to help you."

I looked at Mrs. Darnell. She seemed to have picked up exactly what was going on. What's more, she appeared to be on my side now! She didn't approve of a quest for physical union, but she was more than happy to help me be loved.

"Please," I begged Lane, who was clearly wavering. Why couldn't she just accept that her dream of Shaun was coming true?

I'd been banking on that acceptance. I thought she'd rush to greet it. I'd been wrong, and now all I could do was wait while the balance teetered.

"Well. Maybe just for a minute."

"Great!" I shoved my barstool back and stood up. "Come on!"

Lane slid off hers more slowly. But she gave me a timid glance that I took as being slightly hopeful.

"Thanks." I mouthed the word to Mrs. Darnell as we passed.

"Make sure the door stays open, Shaun" was all she said.

Lane was correct; she was *not* very good at video games. She was sensible about it, though; she didn't squeal or giggle through her mistakes. She seemed to take her poor performance seriously, and I thought she was embarrassed. I sat on the edge of Bailey's bed, observing her closely. I would have preferred it if she were lying naked next to me; still, I enjoyed watching her, even fully clothed. Her face took on that now familiar pinkish tint as she gamely tried and failed to kill alien after alien. Especially when her man on the screen spun around in circles, firing off rounds at his own feet.

Jason snickered on the floor next to her. However, when Lane turned to look at him, he quickly wiped the smile off his face. "Don't worry," he said sincerely. "You'll get the hang of it."

That was the Jason most people never noticed. The one who made an effort to spare someone else's feelings. He was being kind to my darling. I cast an affectionate glance at his back.

Lane put her controller down. "I'm terrible," she said.

"Maybe you should do the tutorial," Jason suggested.

"Maybe you should come sit over here," I said, patting the bed next to me.

"Bailey," Lane said, getting up, "are all those your books?"

"Yeah." Bailey had not been playing, but had pulled the chair out from his computer desk and had been sitting in it, watching Jason and Lane play. Or rather, I thought, watching Lane. I noted that his expression was similar to the one he'd had in the cafeteria yesterday when he'd realized I intended to have sexual intercourse with her.

She went to stand in front of the same shelves I'd perused yesterday. She didn't look at the scattered objects but bent over, looking at the book titles.

"You like Desolation Object?" she asked Bailey

without turning around.

"Yeah." Always the same easygoing tone with Bailey. "Not as much as, say, Tansukai," he added, "but it's pretty good."

Lane straightened. "Tansukai? Do you watch the anime?"

"Yeah."

"Which do you like better, the anime or the manga?"

"Anime. You watch it?"

"Yeah. I like the manga better, though. They censor the anime too much. Plus the English voices sound like California surfers."

"I like the voice for Nakamura, though. He's cool."

"Yeah. And he has some great lines. Did you see the one where he was about to behead Lon and he goes, 'Prepare yourself to feel the wind on your tonsils, dear brother'?"

"I liked the one where he was fighting those two warlords and he says, 'Unfortunately, your intestines will soon be languishing outside your abdominal cavity.'"

"Who's your favorite character?"

"Probably Kohanu or Mina."

"Why?"

"Um," said Bailey, stretching his legs out in front of him. "I like the way Kohanu is kind of a jerk. And Mina fights cool."

"I like The Doctor. I like mysterious, cool bad guys with secret pasts."

Bailey nodded, whether in agreement or understanding I couldn't tell. He said nothing further, but when Lane turned back to his books, he continued to watch her. It seemed to me that his pert, buxom manga girls might be paling in comparison to a flesh-and-blood share-your-interests Lane Henneberger, right here in his room.

Isn't she lovely? I thought, feeling smug. *That's my woman!*

"Let me know if you see anything you want to borrow," Bailey told Lane.

As far as I knew, Bailey had never offered to let anyone borrow any of his books. He guarded them jealously.

Lane gave him a brief glance over her shoulder. "Actually, I was just thinking I wouldn't mind trying the Dead Man Rising series."

"Go ahead and take a couple of them with you, then."

"Or you could stay and read them now," I suggested. "You could lie right here and get started."

"I can't. I have to be home by five."

"Take the first few," Bailey said.

"You sure it's okay?"

"Yeah. Just bring them back whenever you're done and you can get some more."

"Great! Thanks," she told Bailey, beaming as she pulled out three books. "Now I've got to run."

"I'll walk you home," I quickly offered, leaping up. We'd be alone outside, and perhaps I could even hold her hand.

I did, and it was the best thing I'd experienced yet. As we walked up the hill, I reached over and took hold of her left hand, which was warm and slightly damp. Technically speaking, it felt something like a larger, plumper, more flexible version of the hot dogs I'd placed in buns on my first night here.

But as with Shaun's mom, this touch far surpassed its technical components. Her hand was soft, and gently clasped mine in return.

I enjoyed it immensely.

As we walked, I watched the wind toss her hair, and the way her breasts jounced slightly with each step.

Neither of us spoke at first, but as we walked up the hill, Lane said, "There's still something different about you."

I felt my cheeks with my free hand. I wasn't smiling.

"Your eyes look funny. Not funny ha-ha," she added quickly. "But funny different. Like they're . . . I don't know."

"Sparkling?" I asked. I had examined Shaun's eyes in mirrors, and although they were fascinating to me, mostly they were just . . . wet looking.

"Like . . . like there's tons of *stuff* behind them. Experiences." She spoke slowly, as if searching for the correct words. "Happiness. And sadness, too. A *lot* of sadness."

She got all that from shiny eyeballs. "Lane Henneberger," I said. "You are a very observant girl."

We walked up her front steps, stopping before her door. Without withdrawing her hand from mine, Lane turned to me. "I had a good time."

"Me, too."

I expected her to go inside, but instead she stood there, as if waiting for something. I thought perhaps she wanted to see Shaun's smile again, so I obliged her.

"Well," she said, "thanks for walking me home."

"You're welcome," I told her.

Silence.

"So," she said after another moment. "I guess I'd better go in now."

"Only if you must."

"I . . . must." She unclasped my hand and reached for the door handle. "See you tomorrow, then?"

"Tomorrow," I promised, hoping it would be true.

"'Bye," she said. I watched her walk into the house. She *was* beautiful, and I loved her so.

I headed back down the hill, feeling oddly cheerful.

Today hadn't gone at all as I had hoped—yet for some reason I wasn't terribly disappointed.

Probably, I thought, it was because I felt I still had a good shot at achieving the full Lane Henneberger experience.

One more day, I told myself. *All I need is one more day.*

19

Back at Bailey's, Jason was apparently taking a break. He sat on the floor in front of the TV, but was looking around the room, as Lane and I had each done. Bailey had turned on the computer and was playing an online poker game.

I sat on the bed again, leaning forward, elbows on knees, thinking about eyeballs. It was amazing how much some humans could intuit just by looking at them.

Bloo-bloo-bloop! I jumped as a little box popped up on Bailey's computer screen.

I sat up and watched, alert, as Bailey read the words in the box. Surely they wouldn't try to contact me *here*?

Apparently the message was nothing out of the ordinary, because he merely began typing a reply.

I shuddered and looked away.

"You play that?" I heard Jason ask. He was looking at Bailey's guitar.

Bailey glanced over to see what Jason was talking about. "Some," he answered absently. He hit ENTER to send the message, then went back to his poker game.

No more boxes appeared.

I realized now that Jason had introduced a subject of his own accord. I turned my attention to him; the guitar had somehow captured his interest. His gaze moved over its sinuous red-and-white curves. It was an attractive shape, I had to admit.

"You can try it if you want," Bailey remarked to Jason.

Jason looked from the guitar to Bailey, then back again. "You sure?" he asked.

"Yeah. Just be careful."

After another moment's hesitation, Jason gently removed the guitar from the stand. He sat back and cradled it in his lap. Very, very quietly, he plucked a couple of strings, which gave a muted twang.

"Go ahead and turn on the amp," Bailey told him.

Jason leaned over, peering at the knobs. Finally he flipped the switch that said ON. He held one finger over the strings again; then, after another pause, gave a quick strum.

BWONGGGG!

"Sorry, sorry." Jason hastily pressed his hand on the strings, quieting them.

"Just turn it down," Bailey said without looking around.

After a furtive look at me, Jason began to fiddle with the knobs on the amplifier. Then he tried a few more strums, the sound turned so low that I could barely hear them.

It wasn't music, not like the songs I'd heard on Shaun's CD, but it wasn't unpleasant. The notes sounded as if they didn't quite fit where they ought to, but I liked that because it suited Jason, who was, after all, the one making the sounds. This noise was uniquely Jason's, and therefore compelling in a different way from a set of harmonious chords.

I listened to the soft thrum and kept my eyes studiously away from that dreadful computer screen and any potential little boxes.

"I wish I had one of these," Jason said, in a tone of quiet reverence that I would have thought appropriate in a place of worship. But it was clear that he was referring to the guitar. His fingers curled around the neck in what I thought a very natural fashion.

"Borrow Shaun's." That was Bailey.

"I can't."

"Why not?"

"He won't let me."

It was true. Shaun had always refused to let him near the thing. Shaun himself hadn't touched the guitar in a couple of years, but I suppose he wanted to keep it intact in case he ever regained interest. Jason *was* known for his destructive tendencies.

However, *I* didn't care if Jason broke Shaun's guitar.

"Go ahead and use it," I said. "I don't mind."

Jason said nothing, but started strumming the guitar again, as if the matter were of no importance.

Later, though, as we headed home, it seemed to me that he walked a little *twitchily*, as if he was agitated. I wasn't quite certain what it meant. His leg movements were quick, so that I had to walk fast to keep up with him.

As we passed a house with a large chimney that was covered with vines, I remembered that this was the home of the eighth-grader who had much in common with Jason.

I thought: *Here's a chance to make a mark on Jason.*

"You see that house?" I asked him.

Jason squinted at it. "Yeah."

"That's where a kid in your social studies class lives. His name's Carson. He has red hair."

"Oh. Him."

"Yes. You need to go by his house and invite him over."

"What?"

"Right now," I repeated helpfully. "Go ring his doorbell and ask him to come play video games with you."

"No way."

"You're interested in many of the same things. You and he could be friends."

Jason studied the house without slowing. I had no idea what he was thinking. "I don't even know him."

"You will if you go ring his doorbell."

"No. Forget it," he added, with great vehemence. But he was stalking along with long, fierce strides, and I thought perhaps he was *forcing* himself to confront the idea of making a friend. It wouldn't be an easy thought for someone like Jason.

However, when he spoke, it wasn't about friendship at all. "Listen." He sounded angry. "Are you *seriously* going to let me use your guitar? Because if you're messing with me, I'll—I'll—you better not be messing with me."

"I'm not messing with you," I assured him. "You can seriously use my guitar."

"Don't you have a book of chords or something that came with it?"

"Not anymore." Shaun had thrown the book away when he discovered it under his bed, stiff from an ancient spill of some unidentified liquid.

"Oh." One word, but this time the emotion behind it

was clear. Jason's tone was flat with disappointment.

I had never played guitar, but in theory I knew the finger placement of various chords. However, in theory I also knew how to type. The actuality, alas, was quite different.

So I didn't offer any assistance.

Tonight's dinner, unlike previous ones, was rather disturbing. It started when Shaun's mother set a roast chicken on the table. The chicken lay there glistening, and unlike a hot dog or a Quarter Pounder, it had clearly once been *alive*. It still had musculature. And when Shaun's mom pulled and cut loose a leg for Jason's plate, the bones swiveled juicily in their sockets.

I stared, fascinated yet repelled. The thing looked like it could get up and *walk*.

"You want a breast or thigh, Shaun?" she asked me, her knife hovering.

I thought, *If that were Peanut lying there, she'd be screaming her head off.* "What do I usually have?" I asked, telling myself I shouldn't be feeling disgusted. Shaun wouldn't have.

"Huh?"

"Oh. Breast," I said, remembering. "I'll have some breast. Just . . . not much. Please."

She gave me a few small slices, and then served herself. As she and Jason dug in, I poked at the chicken on my plate, undecided whether to taste it.

I tried the creamed corn instead. Yes, that was good.

"Mom," Jason asked, "do you think I could have guitar lessons?"

"*Guitar* lessons?" Her fork hesitated halfway to her mouth. "Um. I don't know. Why the sudden interest?"

For once, Jason didn't shrug. And he actually looked up from his plate. "I was just thinking it would be fun," he said, eyes on his mother's face.

"Out of the blue, you thought it would be fun?" The fork still hovered there.

"He tried Bailey's guitar today," I told her.

"Oh." She began eating again. "But Jason, *you* don't have a guitar. You can't take lessons without pract–"

"Shaun said I can use his."

"*Shaun* said that? Hmm. I didn't know he still had that thing. It's nice of him to let you borrow it."

"So can I?"

"I need to check into it, Jason. I'm not sure how much it'd cost. And the car's been making that funny noise–I need to get it looked at first."

I finished the corn. The small slices of chicken still sat on my plate, looking harmless enough. But before me was the mutilated carcass, cooked muscles hanging in shreds from the skeleton.

I stabbed a green bean and tried that instead.

"I'm through." Jason pushed his plate away. "Can I go get your guitar now, Shaun?"

"Yes." The green bean tasted a little metallic, I thought. Not one of my favorites thus far. Nevertheless, I proceeded to stab and eat more.

"Hey. You be *sure* to put that guitar back when you're finished," Shaun's mother warned Jason.

"I will."

"And be careful with it. And what do you say to your brother for being so generous?" his mother reminded him, but it was too late. Jason was already halfway down the hall.

I ate all the green beans. As I did so, an idea occurred to me.

"You could pay Bailey to give Jason lessons," I suggested. "He'd do it for cheap. He's always looking for ways to make money."

"Or you could show Jason what you know."

"I don't remember any chords," I lied. "Bailey still plays." I had finished all the corn, as well as the green beans. Now I eyed the chicken again.

You're supposed to be Shaun. Just try it.

I slid the tines of my fork into a tiny piece, and lifted it. The meat hung there, white and sinewy.

I stuck it in my mouth and started chewing. Hmm. It wasn't terrible.

"It's really good to see you and your brother getting along," I heard Shaun's mother say.

If you didn't *look* at it, if you didn't *think* about it, it was almost palatable.

"My brother and I were never close," Shaun's mom added as I swallowed my first bite. "It's something I missed."

I deliberately kept my eyes off the decimated corpse in the center of the table and, focusing on my own plate, cut another small piece. "You could try getting close now," I told her.

She shook her head. "Our lives are just too different."

I thought about that. Her brother—Shaun's uncle—was married, with two daughters. He lived one town over. "There's no time like the present to reach out," I said, then ate the second piece.

"You sound like a phone commercial. Anyway, it's not like you're deprived. You get to see your cousins at Christmas."

"I wasn't thinking of my cousins," I told her. "I was thinking of you."

"I'm fine," she said firmly. "Once a year is enough for me to listen to lectures."

"Lectures?"

"Lectures. 'The secret to marriage is that both partners have to give one hundred percent.' The implication being that *I* didn't. That *I'm* a screwup. And that everything my brother does is perfect. Ah, I'm going to get aggravated if I think about it."

I saw what she meant. I considered the matter while examining the chicken that remained on my plate, wondering whether I should try a bit more. "Sometimes," I remarked to Shaun's mom, "people like to feel that any good fortune they have is due to their own wise choices. That's true sometimes, but a lot of the time it just comes down to random chance."

"I'm not following you."

"If your bro— if Uncle Mark likes to believe he can keep bad things from happening to him, then he *has* to believe that the reason bad things happened to you was that you didn't try hard enough." I decided I'd had enough chicken for today. If only it had a different appearance! I'm sure I would have enjoyed it.

When I looked up, Shaun's mom was staring at me with an odd expression. "Wow. Where did all that come from?"

I realized that I'd forgotten to try to sound like Shaun again. I didn't answer, but gave a Shaunian shrug.

"Anyway, you're right," Shaun's mom said. "That's

exactly why I feel uncomfortable around him. I never thought of it that way before." She was silent for a few moments, apparently deep in thought.

"May I be excused?" I asked.

She nodded and watched me pick up my plate, then stack Jason's on top of it. "I noticed you've been putting the breakfast dishes in the dishwasher, too," she said as I reached for Jason's used silverware. "Who stole my son and replaced him with an angel?"

I stopped, hand on a fork, and looked at her.

"My goodness, don't look so alarmed. I didn't mean anything," she said quickly. "What I should have said was that I've noticed everything you've been doing to help lately, and I really appreciate it. You're a good kid, Shaun."

She'd said that last night, too. But I wasn't a kid. And I wasn't Shaun.

"I love you," she added.

I didn't know what to say to that. I just turned and took the dishes into the kitchen without a word.

I certainly liked Shaun's mother well enough, I reflected as I set the dishes in the sink. I just didn't love her as a son would.

I'd already known that, though. Why should the thought seem bothersome now? It wasn't as if I was hurting her by not loving her. Shaun was gone; his place was empty. If anything, I was *helping* his mother by putting off her grief.

I pushed the discomfort out of my head and began to rinse the dirty dishes. I put them in the washer, then headed to Shaun's room to do homework. I could hear Jason thrumming away at Shaun's guitar through his closed bedroom door.

I shut Shaun's door, sat at his desk, and pulled out his English folder. I started working, as I had the previous two nights.

But I'd already run the gamut when it came to selecting writing implements. I'd moved them over the paper in every way I could think of.

Homework was starting to lose its savor.

The assignment was to write definitions for the listed words, then use each word in a sentence. The purpose, I knew, was to help Shaun remember what these words meant.

But I already remembered. There was no point in *my* writing any of it down.

As I pushed the folder aside, there was a knock at the bedroom door.

"Shaun," his mother called softly. "Your dad wants to talk to you."

Shaun usually saw his father one evening a week, and every other weekend. But his father had been on a business trip for a couple of weeks now. So he must be checking in.

I had nothing to say to the man. But the next thing I knew, Shaun's mom had opened the door and was holding out a phone.

I didn't know what else to do, so I took it. Shaun's mom closed the door and left.

The phone wasn't very big, nor was it heavy. Odd, to think that this machine would let my ears listen to sound waves being produced many miles away.

I lifted the phone to my left ear. "Hello?" I said, tentatively.

"Hey, buddy! How are you?"

There were no visual clues at all as to what Shaun's father might be thinking, or even doing. The telephone stripped away all the extraneous physical detail that I'd been enjoying so much.

But because I couldn't see his face, all there was to focus on were variations of tone and volume and resonance. That focus gave his voice shades of emotion that I wouldn't have noticed in person. Even the silences and pauses had meaning. And in just five words, his happiness at talking to his son was almost palpable.

He'd missed Shaun while he was gone; I could hear it in every syllable.

There was a pause now.

"Shaun?" One word, a worry and a question, because I hadn't answered him.

"I'm fine," I said. Then I added: "Dad."

"I missed you guys while I was in Florida. I didn't really have time to sightsee, but I did get to eat at some great restaurants. The seafood was fantastic! You'd love this one place, it was right on the ocean. You could watch the sun set over the waves while you were eating. Sometime you and me and Jason'll go there just for fun; spend some time on the beach, too. How's that sound?"

"Sounds good." That seemed like the correct response.

"So how's school going?"

"Fine."

"You managing to pass everything?"

"Yes," I said.

"You ready to come over this weekend? I thought we could go see a movie. What do you think?"

"Sounds *really* good," I said, trying to express enthusiasm.

"I picked you up a couple of souvenirs, but you're going to have to wait to find out what they are. There's one especially I think you're going to like. I saw it and I thought, *Oh, man, I gotta get that for Shaun!* No, I'm not going to tell you what it is, so don't even ask. It's a surprise."

I felt dreadfully uncomfortable. He was so *glad* to

speak to Shaun. Whom he still wasn't speaking to.

I had already known that for some people, happiness depended on Shaun's being here on this earth. But now it struck me that Shaun had things to offer that I couldn't. He would have been gratified and pleased to see his father for the first time in two weeks. He would have been able to converse with ease, interest, and even excitement. He would have known what to do when his mother put her hand on his shoulder or called him an angel.

He would have known how to respond to an "I love you."

"I know I'm supposed to come get you guys at seven o'clock on Friday," Shaun's father was saying, "but since it's been so long since I saw you, I'm going to see if your mom minds if I come a little early. That okay with you?"

"That'd be great," I said.

"Okay. So . . . everything's all right?"

"Yes," I lied.

"You sure? You're not talking much."

"I'm sure. I'm just a little tired."

"You haven't been staying up too late?"

"No."

"Okay. Well. Is Jason around anywhere?"

"Yes," I said, and added hopefully, "Would you like to speak to him?" I did not like talking to Shaun's father. It was not pleasing.

"Sure. I'll probably see you around five on Friday, okay? Love you."

I did not reply to that. I just carried the phone to Jason's room. When I knocked, the strumming stopped.

"What?" Jason's voice demanded.

I opened the door and held out the phone, as Shaun's mother had done.

Through the half-open door, I could see Jason sitting on the bed, guitar in his lap. He did not move. He looked annoyed at the interruption.

I walked in to hand him the phone anyway, and he took it slowly, as if it might bite.

"Hello? Oh," he said, then visibly relaxed. "Dad. Hi."

I went back to Shaun's room, not to do homework but to sit and think.

I had assumed that a human was bound by its activities and habits, its way of speaking and acting. But now it seemed that there were other threads that wound around someone like Shaun, connecting him to other beings—threads of affection and trust.

Shaun was gone, but his place *hadn't* been quite empty. No matter how I tried to act as he would have, the threads he'd been associated with would always hold *his* unique shape.

Well. It looked like I had just learned something.

Hey! I thought. *Maybe that's why they didn't take me back right away—so that I could learn.*

It was a sobering thought. Might *I* have actually been the focus of a plan from on high?

If it was true—even if the plan turned out to be a minor one that required little thought and no interaction on the part of its maker—it was certainly *very* satisfying.

20

I was sure now that they'd come for me during the night, so I didn't go to bed right away. I sat up one last time, looking through Shaun's high school annual. I tried to imagine what it must have been like for him as he walked down the halls of the school I'd come to know. How it had felt for *him*, looking out of these eyes.

It was quite late when I finally, regretfully, crawled into Shaun's bed, pulled the covers up, and let sleep come.

But when I awoke again, it was a human waking.

I was still lying on Shaun's bed. The hazy feeling in my head, combined with the silence and the dark, told me that it wasn't morning yet; that it was, in fact, the middle of the night.

I quickly became aware that I wasn't alone.

There was someone in the bedroom with me.

I rolled over. Through bleary vision I saw a massive shape in front of the closed door, darker and more menacing than the shadows all around it.

The Boss.

I sat up. I had forgotten what that particular fear feels like. It's a jolt that rips your nerves out of their rightful and accustomed berth.

I didn't mind so much now about being taken away. I just didn't care to suffer on the trip.

My breath felt like a knife in Shaun's body. Stabbing shallow, in and out, in and out. It rattled noisily in the room.

The shape drew closer, towering over me, something between a bull and a man, more powerful than either.

I squeezed my eyes shut.

But once I couldn't see, the air around me felt . . . normal. There was no power in the room. It was an illusion.

There was nothing behind what I saw. Nothing behind my fear.

It wasn't the Boss.

I opened my eyes. The shape was still there, looming like a poisonous cloud.

It spoke.

"You don't belong here." The words came, not from

a throat, but from all of the shape at once, deep and booming.

"I—I know," I whispered, my voice hoarse.

"You can't leave your duties behind," the shadow went on.

But its tone rose oddly at the end. There was something very strange about it. It wasn't doom laden and sonorous.

"You can't just . . . just . . . take off whenever you *feel* like it."

It was peevish, I realized. The tone was *peevish*. *Petulant*.

There was only one unearthly being I knew who would sound like that.

"Anus?" I asked, still not sure.

"Quit calling me that!"

"What are you doing here?"

"It's Anius. An-*nye*-us."

Anius, overseer of the overseers. Middle management of Hell. Just as my function was to reflect sorrow and guilt, his was to reflect anxiety and worry, to fret over dotted i's and crossed t's.

"Why are you here?" I asked him. "What do you want?"

"I'm not talking to you till you say it right."

"An-NYE-us. What are you doing, coming here when

I'm trying to sleep? And looking like *that*?"

"What are *you* doing, trying to sleep? You don't sleep. You don't *need* sleep. You shouldn't be *sleeping* at all."

"I do too need sleep."

"In that body, you do. In that stolen body. And the reason I'm in this form is because *(a)* I don't steal bodies, and *(b)* to show you the seriousness of the situation."

Of all the beings to send for me, they'd picked the one who annoyed me the most. The one I couldn't stand to listen to.

"Wah wah wah," I said, and lay back down, although I was too shaken now to be sleepy. "Go back to Hell. I'm on vacation."

Anius sputtered. "You don't get a vacation!"

"That's why they call it *taking* one."

Anius drew himself up, and the top of him took the form of a shadowy head with horns. "You're breaking about a million rules right now," he said. "You're supposed to oversee the torment of souls."

"That's not a rule."

"Is so."

"It's a *custom*. It's what I've always done. That doesn't make it a rule."

"You know very well that the Creator set us to specific tasks. *My* task is to oversee the overseers. You're making *me* not fulfill *my* function. You're making *me* look bad.

You're going to get *me* in trouble."

"The Creator never set me to any task. Never said a word about anything. In fact, I've never even met Him."

"Oh! Oh! You blasphemer!"

"That's about the size of it, all right. Make a plain statement of fact and it counts as blasphemy."

"You're going to be in such trouble!"

"Oh yeah?" I pulled the covers up under my chin. "From who?"

"From the *Boss*, Kiriel," said Anius.

That opened my eyes.

The Boss. Of course I'd met him; I'd once followed him even to my doom. Beautiful and terrible and endlessly compelling—that was the Boss. Even the thought of his anger a few minutes ago had sent me rigid with fear.

But I had control of my wits again. "The Boss doesn't have much room to complain about *me*, does he?" I pointed out to Anius. After all, hadn't the Boss led the Rebellion, the whopper of revolts, the insurrection to end all insurrections? "And it can't be that important anyway," I added, "if he only sent *you* to straighten it out."

"Nobody sent me. I came of my own accord."

I blinked into the dark. Nobody sent him? Nobody was ordering me to return?

A terrible thought occurred. "Were . . . were you the one IM-ing me?"

"Yes, of course. Who else?"

I lay there, stunned. Could it be that Anius was the only one who'd even noticed that I was gone?

He hadn't come because he was told to. He hadn't even come because he was concerned. The only reason he'd come was out of obsessive worry and attention to detail. That was the only reason he ever did anything.

I sat up again. "You can tell the Boss that I've had it with watching souls suffer. Now go away, you whiny obsessive-compulsive sycophant."

In the dark, two glowing red eyes formed in Anius's head. As if *that* would intimidate me.

I lay down and pulled the covers up to my chin.

"All right, fine," Anius huffed. "Just remember that *I* tried to talk to you. *I* tried to get you to come back. *I* did *my* duty."

"Yeah, whatever." I snuggled deeper into Shaun's bed, as if I were looking forward to the comfort of slumber. "Good night, *Anus*."

When I felt his presence dissipate, I opened one eye. Yes, he was gone.

But after that, I couldn't sleep. I rolled onto my side and lay there, looking at Shaun's wall.

No one had sent Anius.

No one cared if I had learned any lesson. No one had made a plan for me.

No one even felt compelled to protect *my* place in Hell. My identity.

Shaun was lucky. He, at least, would be missed. Shaun Simmons had made a specific mark on his little world, simply by *being*.

A discontent rose in me. I thought, *This must be Envy.* It didn't feel particularly good *or* particularly bad. The only thing about it that seemed even slightly sinful was the way it clung and gnawed, as if it could easily take on a life of its own.

Shaun's pillow cradled my head. I'd stolen a boy's body and the Creator didn't even care! If mankind was of such great import in the overall scheme of things, by George, shouldn't He Himself have shown up to take care of this?

But He hadn't. He hadn't even *sent* anybody.

It was as if nobody was running the universe.

I sat up, punched Shaun's pillow a few times to make it puffier, and lay down again, this time on my back, facing the ceiling.

Maybe the reason no one cares about my absence, I thought, *is that I don't have to be there. Maybe my job is superfluous. Maybe the souls don't really need a mirror.*

I thought about the big reckoning, after the Rebellion. No one told me what my punishment was. I just *knew.* But now I wondered.

Maybe that punishment was entirely self-imposed. Maybe I never *had* to be in Hell, not for a single moment.

Hey. Maybe the souls didn't have to be there either, for that matter. Maybe *their* punishment was self-imposed, too.

Maybe it was a cosmic joke that we'd been making ourselves miserable all this time. Maybe the Creator never really cared about transgressions. Or rebellions.

Maybe He never cared about *me*.

*. . . and the evening and the
morning were the last day.*

21

I stayed awake, thinking, until the silvery light at the window began to take on a faintly golden tinge. Then I got up and took a shower, idly watching my hands run the soap over this body. Yesterday I would have enjoyed the soap's slickness and the way it left a trail of squeaky skin in its wake, but today I was edgy from little sleep, and miffed at the possibility of having been tricked into helping run Hell for all those ages.

I dried off and put on deodorant, clean khakis, a black T-shirt. I combed Shaun's hair.

In Shaun's room, I saw that Peanut had come in and was sitting on the dresser, looking at me. "Ah, Peanut," I said. For some reason I was no longer afraid of him. A cat scratch didn't seem to amount to a hill of beans anymore.

We looked at each other for a moment: the imposter and the only being who cared that he was posing.

He watched me as I sat on the bed, and I watched him as I put on Shaun's oxfords. When I was done tying the laces, I stood, walked over to Shaun's cat, and held my hand out.

"Do you want to inflict a little more punishment?" I asked. "Go ahead, scratch me." I held my hand steady, prepared to feel the razor slash of claws from the only creature in the universe who cared enough to stand up and protect the concept of one's rightful place.

Peanut had been looking at my face, but now he eyed my hand. He didn't hiss, but stretched his neck out slowly, slowly, till his nose touched my fingertip.

I barely felt it: a faint, cool dot, almost not even there, and then it was gone as Peanut settled back.

"What was *that*?" I asked him.

Of course he didn't answer.

"You know I'm not Shaun, and you don't like it. Isn't that right?"

Peanut shut his eyes, as if he'd forgotten about both me *and* Shaun.

"Isn't that right?"

Peanut didn't budge. His sides moved slowly in and out.

"Hey!" I said. "Are you falling *asleep*?"

He was.

I left him there and went to get some Froot Loops.

Shaun's mom had already left for work. I was glad, because I had fallen into gloom. Everything seemed annoying, even though none of it had to do with Anius's visit, which is why I had fallen into gloom in the first place.

Jason came in as I was eating my cereal—I had not poured him any—and as usual, he didn't notice that his brother was no longer here.

Nobody did.

I'll bet I could stay here being human for as long as I want, I thought. *Find out what it's like to age and grow old.*

Jason got his own cereal and sat down with it. He began eating each spoonful in slurps.

I could be his brother for real. If I wanted.

I was surprised to find that I *didn't* want. I liked the kid well enough, and wished him well. I just wasn't interested in a long-term attachment. To me, it sounded dull.

Already some of the novelty of this existence was wearing off—I hadn't even done Shaun's homework last night—and my own actions now seemed to me to be almost pathetic. All alone and unnoticed, playing a little game of dress-up using the clothes of a dead human.

I watched Jason eat and made a decision: I'd give myself one more chance with Lane this afternoon—because I'd really been looking forward to that denouement—and in the meantime, I'd put some final touches on my other projects here.

Then I would exit Shaun. I'd go wherever I felt like going, do whatever struck my fancy.

Hmm . . . maybe body-hopping? I could skip in and out of people as they were going about their business.

What if I picked bodies with a higher profile than Shaun's—ooh, like the presidents of various countries! Then maybe I'd find out exactly what it took to *get a little notice around here*!

"Are you going to Bailey's today?" I heard Jason ask.

"I don't know," I told him. He didn't look at me, but kept his eyes on his bowl as he ate.

If he wants to go, I thought, *why doesn't he just ask? Why does he have to make everything hard for himself?*

"Yeah, sure, I guess I'm going," I said. "Want to come?"

Jason shrugged. "I guess," he said.

My spoon clanked against the bottom of my bowl. I realized I had eaten all the cereal without even noticing. I'd been too busy glooming to experience my Froot Loops.

I was getting entirely too human.

When I got on the school bus, I trudged back to the usual seat by Bailey.

He scooted over to make room. "Hey."

"Hey," I replied, sitting down.

"You get that World History assignment done?"

"No."

"I didn't either. It was hard."

"Yeah," I agreed, although it hadn't been hard at all. Or wouldn't have been, if I'd tried to do it.

As the bus began to move, I caught a glimpse of the driver's eyes in the mirror and realized something was odd about them. In fact, something was odd about the whole driver. She was thinner, for one thing. And her hair was combed in a different style.

Hey, I thought, *that's not my bus driver at all!*

"Who is that?" I asked Bailey, pointing.

"Huh? Oh. A sub, I guess."

"But where's *our* bus driver?"

"I don't know. Sick, maybe. What difference does it make?"

"What difference does it make when *anybody's* not where they're supposed to be?" I asked bitterly. "No difference," I answered myself, slumping back against the seat. "None whatsoever."

"*Okay*. Jeez," Bailey said. "Whatever."

I watched the houses go by. They blurred and ran together like Cinnamon Toast Crunch being poured into a bowl.

"So," I heard Bailey ask. "Are you going to try to get Lane to come over again?"

"I don't know. I guess. Why do you ask?"

"Just curious," he said casually, "since it's my house and all."

Too casually. I turned to study his profile. He seemed to have lost interest in the conversation, and appeared to be looking out the window.

But I remembered how he'd watched Lane yesterday, how he'd let her borrow his books.

As soon as I'm gone, I thought, *he's going to try to steal my woman.*

The bus swayed a little, the engine a low rumble through the open windows. Bailey's face was bland, but his eyes had that far-off gaze I'd already learned to associate with humans in deep thought.

Well, why not? Bailey and Lane were actually rather suited, now that I considered the matter. They had many things in common, and would have plenty of time to get acquainted with each other. Neither had any other prospects at the moment.

After I've finished with Lane, I thought, *Bailey can have her. I hope they bring each other a little happiness.*

Then I turned away and watched the world going by the windows. When we passed the church, I felt an odd bitterness rise up, as if something was clutching at my insides.

I won't take the bus after school today, I decided suddenly. *I'll walk home. And on the way I—one of the Fallen, one of the rejected—will step inside that "holy" place.*

We'd just see if anybody notices *that*.

At lunch I sat with Bailey for the last time. On my tray was lettuce in a rectangular bowl made of paper. On top of the lettuce were crumbles of a grayish meat. On top of that was shredded orange cheese. Next to the bowl was a pile of crispy-looking beige triangles.

In summary: no ketchup. No last taste of the ambrosial nectar.

I poked at the lettuce with my fork, feeling slightly depressed that this would be my last meal as Shaun; I fully intended to be gone before dinner. Bailey didn't seem to mind the food; he downed his chips first and then dug into the salad.

As I lifted some limp lettuce shreds to my mouth, I saw Reed McGowan coming out of the lunch line with his tray.

I'd forgotten about him.

I wasn't feeling too hopeful about having any kind of lasting effect on Jason. There was no telling whether I'd be able to squeeze in sexual intercourse with Lane today.

Perhaps, in the end, I'd have to take comfort in my interactions with Reed. There *was* hope that I had made a tiny mark on Reed's life—a mark that, though small, would remain after I was gone. After all, hadn't I planted the seed of a thought in Reed's head? A seed that might grow, and in the process affect not only Reed, but those he came in contact with?

It wasn't splashy or particularly satisfying. But if everything else went bust, I could cling to the memory of this ex–sower of pain, seeing in him the actual results of *something* I'd done.

I chewed my lettuce and gray meat and watched Reed as he headed in my general direction, bound for the table where his friends were gathered. He picked his way quietly among the occupied tables and chairs, working his way toward his usual spot. When he stood silent and patient, waiting for some girls to move out of his way, I felt my facial muscles relax. I hadn't realized they were tense.

He moved on again, and was coming down the aisle next to me when he had to pause once more for a boy in a wheelchair who was partially blocking the way. That's when he smiled and spoke.

"Move your gimpy ass, you stupid little turd."

I felt as if something actually dropped inside me. As if a weight plummeted behind my breastbone.

The boy, whose leg was propped up in a cast, tried to maneuver his wheelchair out of the way. It would have been quicker for Reed to walk around, but instead he stood there, looming over the boy, whose mouth was drawn tight, whether with embarrassment or anger, I couldn't tell.

The weight seemed to swell up against my lungs.

The Reeds of the world—why did they always feel sorry *later*? Why couldn't they be sorry while there was still something to do about it? All this guy had to do was to keep his mouth shut—just shut up and be still!—right *now*. All Reed had to do was *nothing*.

That was all. And yet he wouldn't do it.

The muscles of my face now felt as if they had gone rigid. And with hardly a thought, as the boy finally got clear and Reed tried to step past me, I turned slightly and put one foot out.

It caught him mid-stride. For a split second Reed's body seemed to stutter in midair—and then it dropped. His tray flew out into a little arc of its own and he landed on top of it, his hands spread on the floor in a belated effort to break his own fall.

"Whoa," I heard Bailey say.

I sat stunned at my own action, looking down at Reed, who was sprawled full length among the chair legs.

I'd always heard of Wrath secondhand. I'd thought of it as a breaking point that comes when a weak container is forced to hold too much. I hadn't realized it rose to tidal-wave proportions in an instant. Or that it squeezed out rational thought in the process.

On the floor, Reed lifted his head. His eyes locked onto me.

I froze.

But as he started to get up, rising to hands and knees, the kid with the broken leg gave one quick glance downward, then backed up just enough to run over Reed's right hand. "Oh," he said to Reed in a tone of surprise. "Sorry."

But then his eyes met mine in a look of sheer triumph.

A wave of laughter began at the tables around me, and grew.

Reed let out a string of curse words—typical American curse words involving the boy's parentage, mental capacity, sexual proclivities, and the inevitable bodily functions.

But that was the extent of his retribution. He rose, kneeling, his face tense, holding his hand nestled close to his body.

I wondered if it was broken.

When he got to his feet, nobody helped him. It was true, what I'd said to him about his friends not liking him. There were a few more scattered giggles in the vicinity, but nobody said anything to him as he stood looking down at the remains of his lunch, on the floor and on his shirt.

Everyone—his friends included—turned back to their food and conversations, and Reed stood alone over his tray as if he couldn't decide whether to try to pick it up.

He didn't. He turned and left, the injured hand still cradled against him.

I sat there as he left the cafeteria. Bailey rose and picked up the tray and silverware from the floor. He didn't attempt to clean up the food, and didn't take the tray to the window. He just stacked it on a corner of the nearest table, came back, sat down, and resumed eating.

That was the only thing anybody did.

I didn't want to eat anymore. I didn't feel one bit better after giving Reed a taste of victimhood. None of the bad feelings in me had been released.

I was weak. I had broken, and without a thought had hurt another being.

I was disgusted with myself.

Was this what being human did to you? Warped you so that all you could think about was the tiny points at which other people's lives intersected yours? Made you forget that every one of these points has not only a history, but an infinite number of possible futures that can be spun out or stunted—or even unraveled to make more possibilities?

All you can think, when you're human, is that Reed McGowan bugs the crap out of you.

I skipped the bus that afternoon, and went to church.

I trudged up red-tiled steps with thin black railings.

There were several heavy-looking dark wooden doors all in a line, and I chose the nearest one.

Inside was a room spreading sideways the width of the building—an entry of some kind, I realized, not the church proper, because before me stood another line of doors. There were windows on each side of this wide hall, and the sun came through so that the white walls, although as featureless in here as they had been from the outside, seemed to radiate a peaceful warmth.

I chose the door directly in front of me, opened it, and walked straight ahead.

The ground did *not* crack open and swallow me whole.

The walls rose high, and when I tilted my head back, I saw that above them floated a ceiling crossed with beams, heavy like the doors, dark and solid against the same calm yet glowing whiteness that I'd seen in the room I'd just passed through.

This was the sanctuary. Was it a holy place?

Yes and no.

This was not the Creator's dwelling place, no more than any other on earth. But the air, the furniture, the walls all seemed to me to be laden with the hopes, the prayers, the love and despair of generations of humans. All that they felt toward their Creator lingered here. And that made the place expand beyond its actual dimensions. I could feel the immensity of it—a tiny shred of the true immensity of the Creator, but immense enough for all that.

There *was* something comforting about it. In some ways it bore a resemblance to bathing in Shaun's tub: the feeling of floating in something thicker than air, something that pressed around me and bore me upward even though I was still on the ground.

I walked a few steps down the center aisle, then stopped. On each side were pews, the backs made of smooth-looking wood, the seats cushioned with a dark red cloth that looked very soft.

I sat on one. It didn't feel as soft as it looked; it was stiff and a little scratchy.

The back of the pew in front of me had a long bin running all along its length. It was divided to hold things. There were empty holes for writing implements. And scattered here and there in the bin were books with red or black covers. I knew what they must be: Bibles and hymnals. I picked one up. HOLY BIBLE, the cover said.

I opened it and started reading.

> One day the angels came to present themselves before the Lord, and Satan also came with them. The Lord said to Satan, "Where have

you come from?"

Satan answered the Lord, "From roaming through the earth and going back and forth in it."

A rather casual, conversational meeting, seemingly contradicting those who call the Boss "the Enemy." As if he is the opposite of the Creator. As if he exists in spite of, and to spite, the Creator's will.

I do try not to think how unfair it all has been. How hard I worked to push aside my nature, wrap it up and lock it away and feel nothing but the pure joy and acceptance that is the Creator's gift to the angels.

But my worship grew to be a burden, not a gift. And so I unwrapped and unlocked the fullness of creation that had been stored inside me.

I was given this nature, but it seems I erred in even acknowledging it, much less exercising it.

Now I shut the book in my hand, sat in the silence, and wondered.

Am I a joke of some kind?

A mistake?

A failure of free will?

A test that was not passed?

One of the aspects of my function is to reflect sorrow. For a long time, I had only felt the sorrow of others. I'd forgotten how blunted and deadened that is, compared to the sorrow that comes from one's own heart.

I had not felt my own sorrow since I truly understood that my Creator would never turn His face to me.

Silence rose, cool and still, into the high reaches of the ceiling. I set the book back into its bin. And then, for the first time ever, I spoke to my Creator in actual words.

"Hey," I said tiredly, into the air. "I'm here." Just putting it out there, just in case. "If You want to get hold of me *personally* for any reason. One on one. This is where I am."

Silence, in this physical world, is not just lack of sound. It's a hollowness that hangs full and thick. It drains the heart as well as the ears.

I knew He wouldn't answer. Not me. He would never speak to *me*. I just thought—well, you know. I thought I'd try.

22

I walked from the church all the way to Lane's house. I couldn't have said what my state of mind was by this time. Much like Shaun's messy room, it was a confusing jumble—of finality, fatalism, and melancholy hope.

The only thing I knew I could count on: *Lane* would notice me. She'd even be *glad* to see me.

On her front porch, I pressed the doorbell.

Nothing happened. No ring. No buzz. It didn't make sense; she had to be here. She always came straight home after school.

I pressed it again, but this time held it down, listening intently.

I still couldn't hear anything.

Apparently doorbells sometimes work even if you

can't hear them. The knob in front of me suddenly turned, the door opened, and there she was.

Lane Henneberger's lovely face broke into a smile. "Oh! Hi, Shaun. I was just thinking about taking Bailey's books back."

"You already read them?"

"Yes. They're good. I'm going to borrow some more."

"Bailey will be pleased."

"I'll get them and we can walk over there together. Just give me a sec; my grandma's taking a nap and I need to leave her a note."

A napping grandma?

Hey! Was I actually having a bit of *luck*?

"Is it okay if I come in for a while?" I suggested.

"Um." She hesitated, with a glance over her shoulder. "Yeah, sure. I guess."

Lane's house was the first one I'd been in that didn't have carpet. The floors were made of wood. Lane had on rubber-soled sneakers that made no noise, but my feet, in Shaun's oxfords, made a hard sound with each step, something between a thump and a click.

In the living room was a huge three-sided couch. It wrapped around the floor like a rectangle with one side missing. Bailey's books were stacked on a low glass-topped table in the middle of the rectangle.

Lane sat on a side of the couch that faced a wall with a

window. When I lowered myself down next to her, the cushion sank in and she tilted sideways, almost into my lap.

"Oops," she said, and readjusted, moving onto a separate cushion. "Are you thirsty? I think we've got iced tea and Diet Sprite. Oh, and water."

"No thanks." I was busy studying her face. I wasn't sure how well I'd be able to recall physical details of this existence once I was out of Shaun's body, but I wanted to try to memorize everything anyway: the pores on her nose, larger than the ones on her cheeks; the way light created white glossy spots that cut across her pupils and irises.

"Um." She smiled, and shifted under my steady gaze. "So. Have you read those?" She waved a hand at the books in front of us. "They're pretty good. There's already some differences cropping up between the anime and the manga. Did you say you'd read the manga?"

"No." I didn't care to spend time on small talk. "Lane. May I tell you something?"

"Sure."

"You're the most beautiful creature I've ever seen."

I thought she looked a little startled. Then her gaze darted away—to the books on the table, to my knees, to the wooden floor. Everywhere but my face. "Let's not do that again," she said vaguely.

"Do what?"

"I *know* I'm not beautiful," she told the floor in front of the couch. "So stop saying it."

It was puzzling. Those words were the exact ones she'd stated—*specifically stated!*—that she longed to hear. "Does it make you unhappy?" I asked, unsure.

"Yes."

"Then . . . I'll try to stop." I watched as a light breeze came in through the open window and lifted the ends of her hair. "It's just that . . . well, you *are* beautiful."

"Shaun," she said with dignity. "Cut it out. We both know that *beautiful* is somebody like Lauren Giotto. Or Sarah Hunter. Or Victoria Becklesworth."

I thought about the girls she meant. "Or Emily Rice," I added. That was the girl Shaun lusted after.

Lane's shoulders seemed to hunch a little.

"I see what's going on," I said. "You're confusing beauty with this society's current idea of perfection of visual form."

She stared at me for a moment. "Perfection of . . . *what?*"

"Visual form."

"'Visual form?'" she echoed slowly, as if trying to understand. "'Perfection of visual form'? . . . But that's what beauty *is*, Shaun."

"You're wrong," I said with finality. I didn't care to dissect the subject at this moment. I wanted to get straight to the matter at hand. To throw myself off the proverbial cliff.

She seemed stiffly surprised when I scooted over and took her in my arms.

Until I kissed her. Then she began to relax.

And soon she was kissing me back.

It felt entirely different from Shaun's T-shirt.

It was amazing. The moment drew out longer and longer; minutes expanded and grew and seemed to wind sinuously around us. Pleasure stretched inside me, growing tighter and more intense as it lengthened, rather like one of the rubber bands in Shaun's desk drawer.

I wasn't sure how much time had passed when Lane drew back with a sigh to rest against my neck.

So. That was a kiss! I could see why she wanted to pause and absorb the pleasure of the moment. That was my darling Lane; she appreciated the things around her.

Her cheek was warm against my skin. "Oh, Lane," I breathed against her hair, "I'm so glad your grandmother's napping. You're going to enjoy this, I promise."

"Enjoy what?"

I was glad now that Shaun hadn't cut *his* hair, because I could feel her fingers caressing it. "Everything," I sighed.

"Everything of what?"

"Everything I'm going to do to you."

Her fingers stopped moving. "What are you going to do to me?"

I remembered that I'd forgotten to tell her I loved her. No matter; she'd asked a delicious and seductive question, one that I had already considered in some detail. "Lots of things," I told her.

"Like *what*?"

"Like—" I began, but then stopped.

Because she was pulling away to sit up.

I didn't have a finely developed instinct for conversation, but it occurred to me that now was not a good time to delineate the methods I'd been mulling over for our mutual journey to sexual climax. Even the really good ones.

I peered into her face. Her eyes were slightly narrowed, the mouth shut more tightly than usual.

"What are you talking about, Shaun?" she asked.

Her tone did not strike me as tender. It sounded more like a warning to me.

"Nothing," I said.

"No, really. What were you about to say?"

"I don't know. I forget."

Lane stared at me intently.

"Shaun. You know I'm not going to have sex with you."

No, I didn't. Lane had spent hours concocting scenarios

with Shaun as the deflowering romantic lead. Now she had him ready, willing, and able. What had gone wrong?

"Your grandmother's asleep," I pointed out.

"Yes, but I'm not . . . I mean, we just *kissed* for the first time."

So what? A lot of people had sex after kissing for the first time.

I didn't point that out, though. Quickly I thought back over what I knew of Lane's desires.

Well. Her writings had—now that I recalled—been very vague when it came to the mechanics of coitus with Shaun. Now that I thought about it, there had always been a leap from about the time he touched her breasts till they lay drowsily together, post-deflowering, in each other's arms. Although Shaun did remove his shirt in many of her entries, the chest she described on him was nothing like the real Shaun's thin and somewhat scrawny build. I didn't recall any scene where his pants actually came off, and there had been zero mention of his sexual organs. Or hers, for that matter.

Uh-oh. Could I have misjudged?

Yes. Most of Lane's expressions of desire had dwelled on the before and after; none had mentioned the *during*. Her imagination had never taken her to any of the places I wanted to explore, and certainly not to the wild dark corners of lust that I was familiar with—

theoretically familiar with, anyway.

Lane had only ever mentioned the most basic wants: to be held, kissed, loved.

I could get those things, or something very like them, from Shaun's bony-handed mother.

Blast! Out of all bodies, why had I taken *this* one? I should have taken one that was already doing all the things I wanted to do.

Of course, I hadn't known what I'd wanted to do until I was already here, but still. It's not like I'm unfamiliar with human desire. I should have anticipated.

"Are you mad?" Lane asked as I slumped back on the couch.

"No," I said. My mouth still felt a little tingly from kissing her. The sensitive skin on my lips must not be used to that particular source of touch, friction, and dampness.

It wanted more. It seemed to have desires of its own now, my mouth did.

And there were other parts of this body that had desires; in fact, Lust incarnate strained at the zipper of Shaun's pants. It reminded me uncomfortably of Wrath, the way it was trying to squeeze out rational thought. It didn't care who got hurt. It wanted to bind me to its will, much as a belt and a pair of pants want to bind an untucked shirt.

So I tried to ignore Lust incarnate. *Okay*, I thought, *maybe lower the sights a little?* We could get similar results without intercourse. We didn't even have to remove all our clothing. It wouldn't be the full experience, but could still end in mutual sexual satisfaction.

"Because I do like you and everything," Lane told me. "It's just that I'm not . . ."

She didn't finish. We sat there in silence for a bit. Sunlight came in the window before us, creating an elongated patch of brightness on the wooden floor.

It felt wrong to be sitting there apart from Lane on this, my last afternoon here.

"That's the first time I ever kissed anybody," I heard Lane say.

I looked over at her. Her face had taken on the pink tinge I adored. "Me, too," I told her.

"Really?"

"Yes."

She opened her mouth, then shut it.

"I liked it," I told her, referring to the kiss. It was true; I hadn't realized how compelling such a thing could be. Each of my five senses had seemed to be mingling with hers, when in reality I was still maintaining a single point of view. It was a truly absorbing experience.

Lane darted a glance at me. "Would . . . would you like to do it some more?" The pink on her cheeks began to turn a pervasive red. "Just kissing, I mean."

"*Just* kissing?" What a shame. There were *so* many

non-intercourse options open to us. "Is that what you want?"

She nodded. The reddish color rose all the way up to her hairline, as if the capillaries had suddenly expanded.

Well. Rather than struggling to clear a route to the sheer peak of orgasm, I *could* explore the myriad delicate facets of making out.

Nothing on this vacation was turning out as I had hoped or expected.

But then, when had anything ever?

I looked outside, at the trees and grass of what must be Lane's backyard. It was a gorgeous afternoon, made so by a million small pieces of chance and imperfection, down to individual tousled blades of grass and small leaves scattered almost carelessly along their branches—everything in its momentary place because of innumerable actions and forces that knit the physical world together.

"You think I'm being stupid, don't you," I heard Lane say.

It's all good, I thought. *Ketchup, tomatoes, just kissing—all of it.*

I turned to Lane. "No, not at all," I said. "I'm quite looking forward to it. Shall we?"

It was some time later when we heard footsteps shuffling down the hall. Somehow we'd ended up lying on the couch, arms wrapped around each other, legs intertwined.

Now we sat up.

Our senses had definitely mingled. Logically, I knew such a thing wasn't possible—but you couldn't tell my tongue that, for example.

"I'd better get going," I told Lane reluctantly as she straightened her blouse.

"Already?"

"Yes. I need to be moving on."

"Hi, Grandma," Lane said in a loud voice as an old woman waddled into the room. "This is Shaun."

"Beg pardon?" Lane's grandmother had fascinating skin. It looked very soft and fragile, drooping and draped over her face. Like lace, I imagined, or cobwebs.

"THIS IS SHAUN," Lane said again, almost shouting.

"Oh. Hello, John. It's nice to meet you."

"It was nice to meet you, too," I told her, standing up. "But I have to leave now."

"What's that?"

"GOOD-BYE," I said.

"Oh, are you leaving?"

I didn't answer, just nodded. I would have liked a closer look at her, but no matter. Lane's grandmother gave a friendly nod back, then began to make her way over to the side of the couch that faced the TV.

Lane walked me to the front door, but when we got

there she seemed to remember something. "Oh," she said. "Would you mind taking Bailey's books with you?"

"I'm not going to Bailey's." A parting gift to both of them. Let her take the books back and get more, and the two of them could bond over their beloved large-eyed cartoon characters.

"Oh. Okay." She opened the door, and I stepped outside—but then we just stood there for a moment, looking at each other.

"Lane!" her grandma called. "Where'd you put the remote?"

"JUST A MINUTE," Lane said. Then she turned back to me. "Well, thanks for coming over, Shaun. I had a nice time."

"So did I."

She dropped her gaze. Her eyelashes were long and lush.

"Lane," I told her. "You *are* beautiful. Believe it."

At that she looked up again, unwavering, her lovely eyes wide and clear, and for the first time she didn't argue. She just smiled again and then, with a long backward glance, turned to head back into her house.

I watched her walk. Her hips swayed with each step, thighs rubbing against each other.

And she didn't think she was beautiful!

23

When I let myself into Shaun's house, his old guitar in its zippered case was standing by the door.

Jason sat on the couch, arms folded. "Where have you been?" he demanded.

"I walked home," I told him.

"Missed the bus?"

"Yeah." The television was off. Jason had clearly been waiting for me.

Ah, Jason. I'd begun something with him that I'd had no intention of finishing. Jason's armor had cracked just the tiniest bit, but when I left this body, that armor would seal right back up, as if I'd never been here.

"Do you want to go to Bailey's again? I asked.

Jason shrugged. "I guess."

"Do you want to bring the guitar?"

Jason glanced back at the case standing there. "Oh," he said, as if the guitar had walked out of Shaun's room, leaped into the case, and placed itself by the door all on its own. "Sure."

Jason's armor, I thought, wouldn't seal itself slowly, but would slam shut in the space of a few words: *Your brother died today.*

"I have a proposition for you," I said without much hope as he rose from the couch. "If you make me a promise, then you can keep the guitar."

"What do you mean, *keep* it? Like, forever?"

"Yes," I told him. "Forever."

His eyes narrowed. "What do you want me to do?"

"Promise that you'll go talk to Carson sometime."

"Who?"

"The kid from your social studies class who lives in the house with the big chimney."

"The one with the red hair?"

"Yes. Maybe you could even invite him over. He likes Tectonic Warriors, you know."

"You mean, go talk to him right now?"

"No. Just someday."

"Someday when?"

"Whenever you choose. You can have the guitar right now, and whenever you talk to Carson will be up to you."

"What about the amp?"

"You can have that, too. Just . . . promise."

"Okay," said Jason promptly. "I promise to do it *some-day*."

"Then the guitar is now officially yours."

I had the feeling Jason didn't think highly of my bargaining skills. He wore the same expression he'd had that first night when he'd caught me with Shaun's shirt. This time, though, he managed to restrain himself from commenting on my mental state. After all, he was getting a good deal.

I knew he had no intention of keeping his word. Still, the seed was planted. And humans *are* known for changing their minds.

"You ready?" he asked.

I shook my head. "You go ahead. I've got one more—something to do here. Then I'll come."

"You want me to wait?"

"No. I'll just be a moment."

I watched him walk out the door. He was the only brother I'd ever had.

The knob clicked behind him. From outside there was a sound much like a guitar case thwacking against a porch railing. It was followed almost immediately by a faint "Oops!"

It's the glitches and twists, I thought, *that make this*

universe unique and compelling. Without flaws, there would be no depth, no substance.

I'd never realized it before. Blasphemy, perhaps—but still, I felt it was true.

Perhaps, I thought as Jason trudged down the sidewalk, the reason I never wanted to worship perfection is that perfection is *dull.*

I turned to look fondly around the living room for the last time. And then I wanted to attend to one last thing.

Peanut.

I found him sitting on the windowsill in the dining room, looking out at the front yard. As I came closer, he turned to stare at me, eyes wide and blank. As usual, I had no idea what he was thinking. If anything.

I approached Shaun's cat and bent over, looking him in the eye.

No sign of recognition. Or hatred. Or disgust.

I extended my index finger, as I had in the morning.

Again Peanut stretched his neck and sniffed my fingertip.

Then he rubbed the side of his face against it.

His fur was soft, like I'd imagined—soft, over the hardness of his little cheekbone. Something about it, about the trusting, pleased way his eyes half closed at my touch, drew a thread of emotion out of me that was pleasing to *me* as well.

Almost of its own accord, my hand rested for a moment on his back, and then began to run along his spine in the direction the fur grew.

His eyes shut completely, and he arched his neck.

And I began to pet him. Immediately a vibration began under my hand. And as I continued stroking and feeling the purr against my fingers and palm, I began to have a melting sensation inside. It was different from Lust, different from what I'd felt with Lane or any of the humans. Softer, milder, more delicate. Quite subtle, actually.

Very pleasing.

As I straightened, Peanut turned to look out at the front yard again, ears forward, suddenly alert.

I followed his gaze. Across the street, a moving van was parked along the curb, dark green like the walls of Shaun's bedroom, doors open and a ramp leading up into the depths of the truck.

Someone was standing on the curb next to it, studying me fixedly.

It was one of the Unfallen.

24

Perhaps I should have cowered in fear. I was too relieved.

Somebody upstairs had finally noticed.

I left Shaun's house for the last time and locked the door behind me. I walked down the sidewalk and across the street, right up to the Unfallen, as if I stopped to chat with seraphim every day of the week.

Hey, did you bring handcuffs? I started to ask, but thought better of it. Unfallen aren't the jokey types.

"Where did you get that body?" I asked instead, looking him up and down.

"It is of my own making," the Unfallen answered, his voice deep and musical, lovely and terrible.

It was obvious that he'd made the body. He certainly wouldn't steal one, and *this* body—well, these guys did not know how to pass as a human.

Bodies have imperfections. This one stuck out like a sore thumb. It was too beautiful. The hair shone, not only from reflected sun, but with an inner light. The skin had a subtle rainbow of undertones that shifted slightly with his breathing and the pumping of his blood. The eyes actually sparkled—yes, *sparkled*—with a fire somehow lit from inside.

The face was completely serene.

This Unfallen's physical form was the most gorgeous thing I'd seen through physical eyes. It certainly had all the working parts.

To me, it didn't hold a candle to Lane's. Or Bailey's. Or Jason's. Or even Peanut's.

"No offense," I said, "but . . . which one are you?" It had been easy to recognize Anius despite his earthly trappings, because of his annoying qualities. Goodness, however, is rather uniform.

"Hanael."

"Oh, yes. Sorry."

He just stood there, studying me with those fiery, brilliant eyes. "Can you read my thoughts?" I asked him.

"No."

"Then why are you standing there, staring?"

"I'm taking pleasure in physical sight."

Well, I knew how that was.

All along I had been unsure about what to expect from this encounter, but it clearly wasn't going to be of the terrifyingly punitive kind. When these guys are in full-blown, wrath-filled I-am-the-messenger-of-the-Lord mode, it knocks you to your knees just to behold them.

I was standing, and quite comfortably. That was a relief.

And now I wasn't in any particular hurry to be whisked away. "Want to sit on the curb for a bit and talk?" I don't get to meet up with Unfallen much. I wanted to feel him out a little, if I could; find out who sent him. Unlike Anius, he wouldn't have come on his own.

"You know that your time here is done. You know that you must return to your proper sphere."

"I know. But . . . let's just sit and partake for a moment, shall we?"

Hanael turned his head, looking all around. "It is a glorious creation, isn't it?"

"Beautiful. It's very . . . layered. I've enjoyed my stay. For the most part." I stepped off the grass and sat on the curb.

Hanael looked down at me. He seemed to be considering.

And then he joined me.

We sat for a few moments in companionable silence. "What is that lovely feeling upon this skin?" he asked after a bit, lifting his face to the sun. "Is it wind?"

"Oh, that. Yes, it's wind—or more like a breeze, really. Hey, Hanael," I said, unable to keep from asking any longer. "Is the Creator angry with me?" Hope springs eternal in a Fallen's breast.

"I am not an intermediary between you and the Creator."

"I'm just asking a question."

"My function does not involve answering that question."

"That's my punishment, isn't it? I am Fallen, and so I'll never get the one thing I crave most—answers. But you, Hanael, you have all the answers, even though you never asked for them or even wanted them. It just doesn't seem right."

"All is right with the Creator."

"Yeah, well, you *would* think so. You're the Creator's Pet, and I'm the guy in the corner with the dunce cap."

"Kiriel. I'm here because you took part of a life that wasn't yours."

"I only took Shaun's body when he didn't need it anymore."

"You took it before he was to leave it behind."

"Just a few seconds before."

"Those few seconds weren't yours to take."

"They would have been filled with pain anyway."

"Nevertheless, they were his. They were not yours. You have interfered with what was to be."

"Yeah, but what can you do? We can't really turn back time now, can we?"

"Shaun will regain possession of his body. He will get those lost moments back. And more. You have interrupted the trajectory of his existence. He requires more time now, to rebuild an arc that is uniquely his."

"You mean he gets to pick back up where he left off?"

"You must leave Shaun's body in the same manner in which you took it."

"Are you saying I've got to step in front of a *truck*?"

"Just so." Hanael nodded. Then he smiled—a lovely sunbeam of a grin. "It's been challenging," he admitted—but not unhappily, it seemed to me. "The man who was supposed to hit Shaun didn't, so his trajectory has to be remade as well. And the woman who will hit him today—yes, you've created some interesting and . . . *unexpected* bits of work."

"But Shaun can't—"

"Shaun will sleep for a while, and when he awakes, his mind's memories of you will be gone."

"You mean, you're going to put the guy into a coma?" I thought about it for a moment. Really, it was probably better than being *awake* for what I was going to do to him.

I thought of exactly what it might mean, coming back to a body that's just been flattened by a truck. "I hope you're going to let him get the full use of his body back," I told Hanael. "It's bad enough that I . . . borrowed it. I've been careful not to harm it—or *tried* not to, anyway—you know, the punch in the face was just a minor bump, not that you'd understand—and now you're going to go and totally bust it up."

Hanael looked amused.

"Okay, I get it. No answers, no hints. As usual. Hey. Stop looking at me like that."

"But I *like* to look at you, Kiriel. You're very interesting—quite an intriguing creation; full of surprising depths, of unexpected twists and turns."

"That's the second time you've used that word about me. *Unexpected*. And you say it like it's a good thing."

Hanael smiled again. "It's a good word."

"*I* like it, but it surprises me that you do."

He didn't argue the point. Of course not: he's perfect. Instead, he said, "Shaun has never appreciated his existence the way you have. Having to work for some of the simple things he has always taken for granted might enable him to be more appreciative, do you not agree?"

"I suppose it might. Just . . . you know. Don't be too hard on the kid. That's all I'm asking. Don't be too hard on Shaun, okay?"

"Are you praying, Kiriel?"

"No, I'm *asking*."

"I'm not the one you should be asking."

I sighed. "I never know if He hears me or not."

"You know He does."

"Well, He never answers me."

"And if you had all the answers you desire, Kiriel—after you received them—what would be left for you to do?"

"Don't be a smart aleck, Hanael. *Capisce?*"

Hanael made no comment—of course not—but merely smiled.

"You smile too much. And quit looking at me like that."

"As you wish. Shall we prepare to go now?"

"I guess." I stood up, brushing off the seat of Shaun's khakis. I looked up and down the street. No traffic yet. "I really loved this place," I admitted. "I wish—I wish—oh, blast. It's going to be like I was never even here."

"You think so, Kiriel?"

"Well, *yeah*. Shaun won't know, like you said. I don't mind that. But there were people—I just wanted to matter a little bit. Leave some kind of mark, the way humans get to. That's all."

"Perhaps you did."

I waited for Hanael to explain, but of course he didn't. It's like pulling teeth to get anything out of these guys. "Like how?"

"Perhaps you should consider the matter more closely."

"Do you mean Jason?"

But Hanael didn't answer.

"Or Shaun?" I realized something. "Because of what I did, Shaun's going to get a second chance. And the people who care about him—really, he's pretty lucky, isn't he? Although I'm sure he's not going to think so, getting hit by a truck and all. He won't know that he was supposed to die. He's probably just going to think his life sucks."

Speaking of which, my last moments here were going to suck, too. "Man, this is going to hurt," I remarked, peering down the street for an oncoming vehicle.

"Yes."

"It's going to hurt bad."

"Yes."

"Guess I can't complain, though. It's part of this existence, pain is."

"Yes."

Two blocks away, a pickup turned the corner and came into sight. You could tell by the way it fishtailed that it was going far too fast.

"Hey," I said, still watching the truck. "Hanael. I've got to ask you something. Did the Big Guy send you?"

"It was part of my function to come."

"But did He send you personally? Did He give you

the go-ahead Himself? Did He tell you to come deal with *me*?"

Hanael didn't look puzzled. That's because nothing ever puzzles the Unfallen. They know all the answers. "It is part of my function to be here," he said, as if that explained it all, "and so here I am."

"Yeah, yeah. I know." These guys are like clocks—you know exactly what time they're going to be chiming before the hands even hit the numbers.

Not me.

A new idea had begun to bubble up. I thought I'd try it out when I got back.

What if I gave some of the souls in my care a teensy nudge or two? Whispered in their ears—so to speak—that perhaps *they* could take mini-vacations of their own? A soul who'd left corporeal existence fairly recently would surely like to pay a comforting visit to a loved one. Souls who'd left the earthly plane long ago might enjoy a quick tour of the places their feet had once trod, to see how things had changed. A particularly weary soul might prefer to merely float in peaceful nothingness, leaving its torments behind for a bit.

Technically speaking, they'd all be breaking a few rules, but what's the worst that could happen to them? Get sent to Hell, ha ha?

Souls are pretty stubborn. But to give us both even an

infinitesimal break from our shared misery—now, *that* would be having an effect!

Even the Creator would surely notice *that*.

I cast a sideways glance at Hanael's shining, obedient countenance, and I knew beyond a doubt that you couldn't *pay* me to be one of the Unfallen.

My place in this universe may not be what others would consider desirable.

But it is *mine*.

The truck rumbled down the hill toward us. It must have been late for an appointment; it was moving too fast. Way past the speed limit.

"They really need to put a stop sign up there," I remarked to no one in particular.

Fear. Horrifying, but when it's the last physical sensation you're going to have, it's delicious. It's a shakiness that starts deep inside, works its way up to your arms, your hands, your jaw. It knots your stomach.

Actually *shaking*! I'm *shaking* with *fear*!

"Catch you on the other side, dude," I told Hanael, and I couldn't help but give him a grin as I stepped off the curb.